For Janet,
Thanks for your
encouragement!
Love,
Carolyn Spangler

Everything GOOD

CAROLYN A. SPANGLER

Inspiring Voices®

This is a work of fiction. All of the characters, names, incidents, organizations, and dialogue in this novel are either the products of the author's imagination or are used fictitiously.

Inspiring Voices books may be ordered through booksellers or by contacting:

Inspiring Voices
1663 Liberty Drive
Bloomington, IN 47403
www.inspiringvoices.com
844-686-9605

ISBN: 978-1-4624-1315-7 (sc)
ISBN: 978-1-4624-1314-0 (e)

Library of Congress Control Number: 2020920110

Print information available on the last page.

Inspiring Voices rev. date: 10/31/2020

DEDICATION

For my two very special sons, David and Brad, who have given me comfort, hope, and encouragement through the years. I love looking at the extraordinary men they have become.

May they both understand that God is by their side through all of life's trials, challenges, and victories.

For the other special people in my life: Don, Bette, Doris, and Veralyn. Thank you for encouraging me, reading my pages, and inspiring me to continue writing.

CHAPTER ONE

EMILY

Everything good comes from God. James 1:17

The Lord is my light and my salvation; whom shall I fear? The Lord is the defense of my life; whom shall I dread?
Psalm 27:1

There's something wrong with me lately. There's an unease at the pit of my stomach. Nothing seems quite right. I should be so happy. I'm wearing Franklin's ring. We're going to set a date, if I can ever decide when. Why can't I just open the calendar and point to a date? Am I afraid? But why? Franklin is kind and gentle; we have so much in common. But what if it doesn't work out? What if I later regret taking this big step? Maybe it'll be another big mistake. I have a problem. I need help.

Emily Sanderson sat at her desk, in Room 41 of the English hallway, munching on M&Ms as she read one of the mystery stories her third hour class had handed in that morning. It was good. Very good. The kind of story that made her feel satisfied with her job as a teacher. So good she had forgotten how many M&Ms she had just chowed down.

She'd regret it the next morning, for sure, when the bathroom scales scolded her. But she needed something to keep her going for a while, at least until 5:00. Then she'd have to go home and figure out what she and Katie would eat that night.

She paused from reading and looked around the room. It was a comfortable place for reading. Posters on the wall about exciting novels to dip into, a vase of tulips on her desk, a corner book case, and an easy chair for students to lounge in when they had an extra moment. She liked her room, loved her job, and generally felt at peace. Well, sort of. It would be better, she was sure, once she settled the issue of Franklin and marrying. Marriage the second time around could be scary. What if it was a disaster like the first time? Or again, what if it was hundreds of times better?

Then Emily looked down at all the waiting papers; she could have lugged all of them home, but she thought if she got some out of the way now there would be fewer to stare her in the face that night. And Tom was coming home from Chicago this weekend. She always looked forward to seeing her son and wished he lived closer. She was hoping there would be lots of time to discuss his future plans; he had hinted at some changes coming up.

Emily glanced out the window at the clouds and hoped snow wouldn't come again this weekend. It was almost spring. The weather man seemed to have the seasons mixed up lately. The problem was the road between Chicago and Springton, where Tom would be traveling. Right at the bottom of Lake Michigan. It could be windy and treacherous if it was snowy.

She picked up the paper again. The girl in the story had just discovered a body. A surprise. Good for the author, Emily thought. She, the reader, hadn't seen it coming. She finished the story, jotted a few positive notes on the paper, and gave it an A.

Then she came to Marco's story. It felt thin; it was. Only three pages long. Not a good sign. As she read, she found it to be about a father who had left the country without telling his family why. Marco wrote a note at the end saying that he had had no time to finish because of family responsibilities. Hmm. What was that all about?

Just then Emily heard a key unlocking her classroom door. She put the story down, startled, and wondered why no one had knocked.

Ralph, the custodian, peered around the corner, looking as surprised as she felt. "So sorry, Mrs. S.," he said. "I really need to clean the room."

"Could you give me half an hour?" Emily asked. "Then I'll be out of your way."

Ralph frowned as he pulled his gray shirt down over his protruding belly. "I suppose so. Hope I don't forget." Then he backed out the door.

You better not forget, Emily thought. Sure wish we had Jose back. He was so much nicer than grouchy Ralph with the scraggly brown beard. And the attitude, like he was too good for the job. Which could be true. He seemed much older than most of the custodians. Anyway, Jose would have stopped to chat and even ask why she was working so hard and so late.

Jose. Emily thought back to Marco's essay. Jose was Marco's dad. Interesting. Was Marco writing a story about his dad?

Unfortunately Jose had temporarily left at Christmas break. His mother, who still lived across the border in Nogales, Mexico, was ill with cancer. Jose hadn't seen her in years because of all the problems crossing the border. He had to end up going by himself, since his wife couldn't leave the country and ever expect to come back. Jose hated to leave her and the kids behind, but he really needed to see what he could do to help his mother. Fortunately the school had agreed to hold his job open for as long as he needed.

How he must miss his family, Emily thought. And how Marco must miss his dad. She hoped that someday the laws would change to help people like Jose. She didn't know their entire story, but she suspected his wife had come illegally to the U.S. years ago, perhaps as a youngster.

Emily shook her head as she wrote a comment on his story. "Good start," she wrote. "It sounds like there are many problems to solve." And then she added this: "Come and see me; let's talk about how you could finish this."

Her problems seemed minor after thinking about Marco and Jose. Suddenly she heard what seemed to be angry whispers in the hallway. She looked over at the door in annoyance. It would be so nice to finish just a little more before heading home. Naturally Ralph hadn't closed the door all the way. She walked over quietly to see if she could tell what was going on.

"I'm getting sick of your blackmailing me," the person said, obviously trying to not talk too loudly.

"Who cares," Ralph snarled at the other person.

Who was Ralph talking to, Emily wondered. Another custodian? Surely not a teacher. For some reason she couldn't move. She didn't really want to hear the conversation, but it might look funny if she suddenly closed the door.

"I just don't have the money now. I'll get it soon."

Sam. Emily thought she recognized Sam's voice. He was a custodian in the freshman wing; what was he doing over here?

"One more week," Ralph said. "And then watch out."

"Look, I came all the way over here to talk to you; can't you give me a chance?"

"One more week."

Then she heard footsteps stomping off down the hallway.

Emily walked back to her desk, thinking she'd had enough for one day. She wouldn't be able to concentrate after what she had just heard. Might as well go home.

⁂ ⁂ ⁂

Later that evening Emily and Katie cleaned up the kitchen after making BLT sandwiches.

"I hope you aren't too hungry after having only a sandwich. I promise I'll make something better this weekend," Emily said as she stacked their plates in the dishwasher. She looked at Katie carefully. Other than appearing tired, one would never know she was about two months pregnant. Except for the morning sickness. She knew that Katie still carried saltine crackers in her bag for those touchy moments.

Katie smiled tiredly and brushed her bangs out of her eyes. "No problem, and I really love BLT sandwiches." She sat down at the table that stood at the side of the small kitchen. "I appreciate your not asking me every night about what's going on with Dan and me."

Emily sat down opposite her daughter and started folding the napkin that had been left on the table. It had been incredibly hard not to ask questions. She worried about Katie. Of course she worried about her only daughter, who was pregnant and unmarried. How could she not worry? Except she knew it wouldn't do any good. She heard at church over and over about how she needed to put her problems in God's hands. She just needed to pray, and He would handle things in His own way and in His own time. Nothing would be gained by worrying.

Dan and Katie seemed to love each other. A baby was coming in November. Wasn't it time for a wedding? Emily put an invisible clamp on her mouth. This was their problem, not hers. She just smiled encouragingly.

"We're going to talk again this weekend, and finalize plans. There have been so many decisions to make . . . We'll let you know very soon."

"But . . ." Emily hesitated. "A marriage, right?"

"Yes, for sure." Katie stood, gave her Mom a hug, and trotted off to her room.

Emily watched her retreating back. Her beautiful dark-haired daughter was all grown up. When had it happened?

How ironic, Emily thought. Both she and Katie were having problems setting a date. Franklin had said that this weekend they should do some planning. Emily sighed. Then she prayed her thanks, and also prayed for the strength to help Katie however she could.

❋ ❋ ❋

The next morning Emily drove her car into the teachers' parking lot and wondered why snowflakes were drifting down. It was March, for heaven sakes. With spring so close, this snow just didn't seem right. She parked, pulled her heavy Vera Bradley briefcase out of the back seat, and hurried to her classroom. It would be good to empty the case of all the mystery stories. She had stayed up late and almost finished reading them before falling asleep at the table. Only three more left.

She unlocked and opened the door, then switched on the light. And gasped. It was chaos. A total mess. Student desks were turned over. Her teacher's desk, usually full of books, pens, a stapler, a vase of flowers, a lamp, etc., was empty. Everything was strewn all over the floor. A bookcase, usually full of novels, was on its side, with all the books underneath.

Emily stood at the door, in shock at what she saw. Why? What did this mean?

"Emily, you're finally here," Franklin called from down the hall. He came up to the door, looking bewildered at her standing in the doorway. Then he saw why. "Good grief. Looks like a party gone bad."

"I can't believe this," she said. Who could have done such a thing? Was someone totally upset with her? A student?

Franklin walked in, looked around, and seemed to be making a decision. "Let's lock the door and go to the office. Steve needs to know about this right away." Franklin took the key from her hand, locked the door, and led her by the arm down to the assistant principal's office.

As they walked down the hall, Emily felt protected somehow by this man she had come to love. She liked the way he had seemed to know just the right thing to do. She looked up at his kind and determined face and thanked God again for bringing him into her life.

⁂ ⁂ ⁂

Emily had quite the story to tell Tom when he drove in later that night from Chicago, around 8:00. He looked good in his khaki slacks and blue sweater.

"Hey, Mom. How was your Friday the 13th?" Tom called as he walked in the front door.

Emily turned off the television. She had been watching some inane comedy, hoping to distract herself from the events of the day. "Oh yeah; I guess that explains today." She tried to laugh, but the mess in her room was still too real. It was hard to believe that someone could do that to her. Maybe she shouldn't take it personally, but she did.

Tom dropped his suitcase off in the bedroom, went to the kitchen for a soda, and then flopped down on the sofa. "So, a bad day?" He kicked off his shoes and sat waiting for her answer.

Tom, the older of her two kids. Tall, like her father had been, and slender. She loved the way he asked a question and then actually looked like he wanted an answer. Unlike some kids who never seemed interested in their parents.

"And how." She described the classroom as it was that morning. Steve, the assistant principal, had her first and second hour classes meet in the library while George, one of the day-time custodians, cleaned up her room. He had done a super job.

"Was yours the only room?"

"Actually, no. There was one in the math wing, also."

"So did they discover the culprit?"

"No. Steve called the police, though, and they looked through the rooms before they were cleaned up." Emily got up to close the blinds, as it was completely dark now. Then she switched on the gas fireplace. "Will this be too warm, Tom?"

"Oh, no. Feels good."

She sat down near the warm fire and once again thought how thankful she was to have this fireplace in her home. It made it cozy, like an oasis in a dark world. Especially a world where someone would invade her very own classroom. She shivered, feeling spooked that someone had looked over her things and thought to do such damage.

"I quit my job," Tom announced with a smile on his face.

"You did what?" Emily stood up suddenly.

"I quit my job, but everything is okay. Don't worry."

Another thing not to worry about. Great. Just great. She wondered, again, when one stopped worrying about her kids. Maybe never. "Well, this is quite a bomb shell. I'm going to the kitchen for something. Wait here."

Tom chuckled. "Did you bake after school?"

"Yes. Be right back." Of course she had baked. It had helped get her mind off the "invasion" as she thought of it. Not that she'd really forget it that easily. Still . . .

A few minutes later Emily emerged from the kitchen with a tray of chocolate chip cookies and a Diet Coke for her, since Tom had already found his favorite root beer soda. "I figured we needed goodies for this conversation. So tell me all about it."

Tom reached for a cookie and began. "Actually there's not lots to tell. You know I haven't been all that happy at the golf company. I've been asking questions at the hospital, and the personnel director called this week. Said they could use me full time until I go back to WMU for classes next fall. So after thinking it over for about a minute, I gave my notice today, and said I could work two more weeks if they'd like."

"Wow," Emily said. "A big step. I probably shouldn't be surprised. What did your father say?" Emily had a feeling that Jack, her ex, wouldn't like it one bit that Tom was resigning. Jack was also a salesman for the company and had gotten Tom the job in the first place. She knew he had enjoyed having Jack nearby. And she couldn't blame him. But if Tom wasn't happy selling golf clubs, it was certainly his right to move on.

Tom glanced her way. "He was predictable. Wondered if I was being pre-mature, that I could have made lots of money before classes next fall."

Emily nodded, imagining the conversation between Tom and his dad. Jack knew everything, or so he thought, and was always right. Tom seemed to know how to handle him, though. Also, she knew how Tom had never really liked being a salesman for the golf company. Emily guessed that there weren't enough challenges there. Working at the hospital was right up his alley. Maybe this was all working out for the best.

"So, one more thing," Tom said. "Is it okay if I settle in the third bedroom again?"

"Oh, Tom, of course it's okay."

"Of course I'll be at Western in the fall; I'll get an apartment there and just come back on weekends perhaps. Anyway, this won't be permanent."

"This is always your home," Emily said.

CHAPTER TWO

TOM

Turn to me and be gracious to me for I am lonely and afflicted.
Psalm 25:16

When Tom Sanderson turned into the parking lot of Springton General Hospital that first Saturday morning in March, he sighed with relief. It was good to see the rather old brown brick building. It felt like coming home. Sure he had only worked here part time before, mainly Saturdays, during his time in Chicago for the golf company, but it still felt right. No golf clubs to lug around today. No filling out orders for stores who bought more supplies, but didn't really have an urgent need for them. People needed him here at the hospital, sometimes urgently needed him. He could be of use, help someone. The personnel director of the hospital had even given a name for his job – nurse helper. Tom liked it. Yes, he had been right to quit his sales job at Golfing Unlimited. With any luck at all, they wouldn't need him to stay the usual two weeks.

Tom parked, checked his watch, and saw that he was early. He'd just sit a minute. He definitely was glad to be working at the hospital again, and he thought of all the changes that were coming in the fall. He'd be going to Western Michigan University and working on his master's degree, along with a secondary teaching certificate. That was a huge change from years ago when he had thought medicine would be the career for him. That was before his divorce, and before his diagnosis of Parkinson's, which had turned out to be false. That had been a very low point in his life. He had felt so lonely and depressed. His dad had suggested working at the golf company in Chicago while he figured out what he wanted to do with his life. Or maybe that would indeed be his life. He had been so unsure of himself for a while, so it had been a good change. Now, though, he wanted to teach history, much like Franklin, he mused, and work with kids. That sounded good to him.

Finally he opened the car door, walked across the parking lot and into the double wooden doors of the hospital. First he'd head to the staff lounge to shed his heavy winter jacket. Tom opened the door to the lounge and noticed Stella, surrounded by three other nurses. Pretty as ever. He and Stella had dated a few times; she was fun to be around, but he had a feeling that was all it would ever be. Now she seemed to be telling a story. He waited at the door so he wouldn't interrupt.

"No, I don't do church. What do people get out of it anyway?" Stella asked the others.

"Beats me," the redhead said. "It's boring and you feel guilty for not being there all the time."

"I've got a funny story about that," Stella said. "A Sunday school teacher asked the kids a question. Why should we be quiet in church? A little girl said that it's because people are sleeping in there."

"Sounds like my parents' church," said one nurse, and they all laughed.

Tom closed the door and Stella looked his way. "Hey, Tom. Good to see you."

He waved as he walked to the coffee pot. Apparently they hadn't noticed him listening in on the story. Good. Better that way. The part about people sleeping in church was a bit funny, though. And unfortunately true. Sometimes a sermon could be boring. A church is filled with all kinds of men and women his pastor had said one Sunday. It isn't a place for perfect people.

As he poured cream into the coffee, he thought about Stella's church comment. It seemed to confirm what he had felt earlier, that she wasn't very comfortable with the idea of going there. She must have tried it once, as she seemed to indicate, but had found it boring. No doubt that was why they hadn't really clicked before, when they dated a couple of times. He wanted someone, someday, to be as committed to church as he was.

He put a lid on the cup, hung up his jacket, and walked toward the door.

"Tom," Stella called. "Wait up a minute."

He waited, and they walked down the hall together. "Some of the nurses are getting together tonight after work. Care to join us?"

He glanced her way; he still found her attractive, but, no. "Sorry, Stella. I can't tonight. But thanks for asking." She looked disappointed. "I just got home from Chicago last night, and Mom is planning a big dinner." Well, there had been a time when he would have welcomed the invitation. Not now, though. He had come to the realization that compatibility is crucial in a relationship.

Fortunately they saw Nurse Cheryl in the hallway; she called his name right then and asked him for help in Room 45. "Sure. Be right there. I'll just tell the front desk what I'm doing."

He and Stella parted. He hadn't lied. He really couldn't tonight. He had promised his Mom he'd be home for dinner. But he was glad for an excuse. It didn't seem like he and Stella had all that much in common, contrary to what he had thought at first. Had he been that lonely? Enough to overlook so many differences? But that was okay. He had too many other things to worry about right now. Right?

❋ ❋ ❋

Tom checked in, then walked quickly toward Room 45. Cheryl had sounded a bit frantic.

"Tom, over here," Cheryl whispered as she stood outside the room.

Tom could hear yelling from inside the room. "What's going on?" he whispered back.

"The patient is Jared. Gunshot wound to his shoulder. He found a Bible in his room and he wants it out. He keeps yelling bad things about Christians."

"Run down to the cafeteria and bring a Coke and some cookies," Tom said. "Hurry!"

Tom opened the door to find a young black man standing beside the bed, ripping pages out of a Gideon Bible.

"Trash, trash, trash," he kept shouting to himself. "Lies, lies, lies."

"Jared," Tom said as he walked in and started picking up torn pages. "What's the problem here?"

"The nurse wouldn't get rid of this stupid Bible, so I just decided to do it my way."

"Makes sense," Tom said calmly. "Here, give it to me and I'll throw it in the hall."

Jared looked up from his tearing as if he were surprised at Tom's logical, soft voice.

Tom hoped his acceptance of the tearing would calm him down. He wondered what in Jared's past had made him so distraught about seeing a Bible in his room. An over-bearing father, perhaps? A mother who had forced him to go to Sunday school? "It looks like you've got quite a problem with your arm. Let's get you back on the bed while I get rid of this book for you."

Jared sullenly gave him the Bible, then let Tom help him back on the bed. Tom quickly walked to the door and threw the book out. Fortunately Cheryl was just coming with the Coke and cookies.

"Thanks. And could you get rid of the Bible? Maybe take it to the lounge," Tom whispered.

She nodded and scurried off.

'You don't happen to like chocolate chip cookies do you?"

Jared nodded. Tom pulled the tray to the bed and deposited a plate of cookies and a Coke on it.

"Would you like coffee instead of Coke?"

"This is okay."

"Have you been here long?" Tom asked.

Jared nodded as he took a huge bite of a cookie. "A couple of days. Surgery on my shoulder." He seemed much calmer now, which was good.

"Sorry to hear it. Do you need anything for pain? I could get a doctor to come in."

"Nah. It'll be okay." He seemed to think a minute. "I just need to get out of here and back to work." Jared rubbed his eyes and sighed. "They say I'll be here a few more days."

"Sounds tough," Tom said. "What kind of job do you have?"

"Just Young's Sporting Goods on Main. A clerk. I'm hoping they'll hold the job for me."

Just then another nurse came in to look at his shoulder.

"Care if I check on you later?" Tom asked.

Jared nodded. "Whatever." He turned to the window with another cookie in his hand.

Tom left the room and walked over to the nurses' station to ask Cheryl more about Jared. "Any idea how Jared got shot?"

"I heard he was wrestling with a guy who wanted to rob the store where he works."

"And did the robber get away?"

"That's the thing. He's actually something of a hero because he held the robber on the floor until the police got there." Cheryl sounded impressed.

"Good for him," Tom said. But he still had quite a wound, and no doubt lots of pain.

⁂ ⁂ ⁂

Tom left the hospital late that Friday night, glad that he could just go back home and relax instead of going to a party. But first he had gone to Young's Sporting Goods Store to ask about Jared's job. Normally this wasn't expected of a hospital worker, but this seemed important enough to do on his personal time. And he was glad he did it, because they were more than willing to hold the position for him. Tom would be able to take good news to Jared tomorrow.

But the whole day had been busy, with many patients needing some kind of help. Robert in 205 needed a shower and Mrs. Dane in 301 had to be transported to surgery for her foot. Little Amy in the kids' wing had been crying because her mom couldn't come to visit. Cheryl had tracked him down and asked him if he could help.

"Do we have any kids' books in the hospital," he had asked her.

She shrugged. "Beats me. Maybe in the gift shop. But Tom, she's getting hysterical. She needs someone now."

He had hurried to her room, wondering what he could say. Kids weren't really on his radar these days. Not that they ever had been. Even when he had been married before, kids had always seemed like something he and his ex. would have in the far, far future. He had always felt a bit awkward around them, which had happened when friends with kids came to visit his mom. Then he saw a Cinderella kind of figure on the wall. Maybe he could remember that story and tell it to her.

"Hi, Amy. I'm Tom. Good to see you. Can I sit with you for a while?"

She nodded, sniffling, clearly surprised to have someone paying attention to her. She must have been only five or six, he thought. Cute, with soft brown hair in a ponytail.

"I just saw a picture of Cinderella on the wall outside. Actually, I think you look just like her." Tom smiled as her face broke into a grin. "Do you know that story?" He propped open the room door and pulled up a chair beside her bed.

She just nodded again. Tom found a tissue box and gave it to her. She pulled one out and wiped her face.

"Shall I try to tell you the story? But the problem is that I don't think I remember everything. Maybe you could help me if I forget."

She gave a little laugh. "Everyone knows about Cinderella."

He raised his hands if he were just stupid. "I know, I know, I should know it, right?" Then he started telling the story, with much help from her.

Cheryl came in with dinner just as they finished and were talking about the mean step mother. She winked at Tom. "Thanks," she whispered.

"I have to leave soon, but I could stay with Amy while she eats dinner, if you'd like."

Amy clapped her hands. "Please stay!"

"That would be great, Tom. And Amy, I'll come back soon. Maybe we can find something for you on TV."

❋ ❋ ❋

"So that's the story of my day," he said to his mom as they ate chili that night.

"You seemed to have a good one," his Mom said. "I'm wondering about Jared. He sounds like a hero for the store."

"He sure was; he was able to tackle the guy and hold him until the police got there." Tom thought a minute. "In spite of that, he's really hurting, and very mad at God. I'm going to look in on him tomorrow before I go back to Chicago. At least I can tell him that he'll have a job to go back to."

"Tom, that's huge. He's bound to feel better when you tell him," Emily said. "And just your showing up and being a friend could be exactly what he needs."

CHAPTER THREE

KATIE

> And we know that God causes all things to work together for good to those who love God, to those who are called according to His purpose.
> Romans 8:28

"Aren't you the clever one, the way you made up lies so he'd have to marry you. Good job."

Katie Sanderson looked around her little corner of the college bookstore, trying to see the voice behind those hateful words. From where she was putting away Freshman English textbooks, all she could see was a long stack of books. So she walked to the end of the aisle and came face to face with Angie. Not exactly her favorite person on campus. Angie, who went to Dan's church. Angie who always looked slim and pretty with her perfect blonde hair pulled back in a neat ponytail, and dressed in expensive jeans and sweater. Angie, who had made it clear to Katie that Dan was hers. All hers.

"And now," Angie continued in a low voice, "he may not ever get to be the missionary he has always wanted to be. And all because of you. How selfish. I bet it's not even Dan's baby." Angie finally finished her rant, flipped her ponytail, turned around, and walked out the door.

Katie just stood there looking after her. Stunned. Had that really happened? Maybe she had imagined it. No. No mistaking the frown on Angie's face, the loud voice, the finger pointing at her. How could anyone be so mean and hurtful? And Angie went to church. She had always assumed that was where people learned how to be good. Maybe Angie still had a lot to learn. Is this what church people were really like?

She glanced around, wondering if anyone had heard Angie. The only person she saw was Buddy, who was standing behind the cash register reading a sports magazine. Apparently he had been too engrossed in a story to hear anything around him. It had been a slow Monday, for which she was grateful. And Dan was out at the warehouse picking up a new supply of American history books. Angie must have known he wasn't there; surely she would never have talked to Katie like that otherwise.

Katie walked over to the book corner, a cozy place with two comfortable chairs, a round oak table, and a floor lamp. Sometimes students took advantage of this little corner to quietly read. It looked very inviting right now.

As she sat down, she realized that Angie had struck a nerve. Katie hated to think that Dan, the manager of the college book store, would have to give up his dream of doing missionary work. It had been bothering her a lot lately. He had planned on starting Bethel this semester, getting a master's in ministry, but had cancelled when Katie became pregnant. Money. That was the problem. To get married and support a family, he would have to keep his bookstore job and put off going back to college. But if Katie were out of his life, he could go to Bethel next fall.

Katie sighed. She had told her mom this past weekend that she and Dan would be making decisions soon. Very soon. But she and Dan hadn't even talked about it when they went out to a movie Saturday night. They had seemed content to laugh at the movie and enjoy each other's company. But was Dan having some second thoughts about being tied down with her? And then Sunday morning she'd had a bad case of morning sickness, so she hadn't gone to church with Dan. She was sure Angie had taken her absence as a sign that she hadn't completely lost Dan yet. Angie had no doubt taken the opportunity to talk and flirt with him. She was like that.

❋ ❋ ❋

Now, sitting by herself in the book store, Katie felt tears come to her eyes. Maybe Angie was right; she, Katie, was selfish. Dan needed to go back to school; he needed to be the missionary he had always dreamed about. This baby would take all of that away from him. He'd be stuck in this book store forever, because of their one mistake.

She wiped tears from her face and onto her old inexpensive jeans and got up with determination. Something had to be done. But what? That was the big question. She went back to shelving text books, deep in thought. So deep that she didn't hear Dan come back from the warehouse.

"Hi Katie," Dan said as he put an arm around her.

Katie jumped and turned out of his embrace. This is it, she thought, carefully not looking at him. If she looked in his eyes, she'd change her mind. But she had made a decision and had to go through with it. She knew she had to let him go.

"Dan, we have to talk," she said as she studiously looked at the text books.

"Sure. Let's go in the office. Is something wrong?" Dan led the way to his tiny office, turned on the light, and closed the door. Then he took a stack of books off of the extra chair, motioned for her to sit, and sat himself on the edge of the desk. "Are you feeling all right? Are you getting too tired to work?"

He looked so handsome this morning, in a navy sweater and khaki slacks. The love in his eyes made her heart melt, but she had to be strong. She had to think of him, of what was best for his future, and not be selfish.

That was her opening, she suddenly decided. "Well, I have been awfully tired lately. I'm thinking I should quit." She rubbed her hands together, feeling anxious. It was a little white lie. Just a little one. She really did get tired more easily lately. Dan knew about her awful morning sickness. Maybe that made her supposed tiredness more believable.

"Okay," Dan said. "Then you should definitely quit. In fact, I should have thought of it before now. I'm so sorry."

"Oh no, that's all right." She paused. "But there's more."

"More? Katie, what is it?" Dan scooted his desk chair next to her and took her hand, rubbing it gently. "It's the ring, isn't it? I said I'd be getting you one and I haven't yet. But I will. Really. In fact, maybe we could go shopping together, tonight."

"No, Dan. It's not about the ring. That's not important." Then tears, those stupid tears, came to her eyes again. What could she say to set him free? Suddenly she stood up. "I'm sorry, but I can't do this. Get married.

I've changed. I just don't feel that way about you anymore." With that, she fled out of the office, found her coat and purse, and ran out of the book store.

"Katie, wait. Let's talk."

She heard him call, but ignored him as she rushed to the car and drove off. What have I done, she thought, brushing tears away so she could see to back out of the parking space. What am I doing to my life? What will happen to me? And the baby. Yes, there was a baby coming. She had plans to make. Others had done it. She could, too.

※ ※ ※

Katie barricaded herself in her room, crying into her pillow so her Mom and Tom wouldn't hear. She had told them, through the door, that she was going to rest because she didn't feel well. And no, she didn't feel up to any spaghetti tonight. So they left her alone. While in her room she heard the doorbell ring, then her mom talking to Dan. Her mom convinced Dan to let Katie rest. Thank you, Mom, she thought to herself through her tears. Yet she wanted so much to see him and feel his arms around her. Was she doing the right thing? Was all this pain right? Yes, of course. It had to be. She was thinking of Dan, of his future. And then more tears.

The next morning she dragged herself out of bed; she had four classes at community college that day, and tests in two of them. Fortunately her Mom and Tom were up and out of the house before she got up. She couldn't stand to have them hovering over her and asking how she was. Truthfully, she didn't feel well. Her morning sickness seemed worse than ever, even after she ate a couple of Saltine crackers. She dressed in her old jeans and an extra-large shirt to cover up any bumps that could be noticeable, and drove to class.

It was during her first class that she realized she had made a big mistake by coming. The test questions were hard; she couldn't remember anything. Then she started having more stomach pains.

She finally gave up thinking about the questions and went to the teacher's desk. "Here's my test; I'm sorry, but I'm not feeling well. I've got to leave."

The teacher nodded an okay, and Katie left. She walked down the hall to the front doors, opened them, and sat on the bench outside. The pains weren't going away; just the opposite. What was going on with her?

When she couldn't stand it any longer, and didn't think she could even make it to her car, she took out her cell phone and called Tom. "Is there any way you could come and pick me up? I don't think I can make it home." And then the tears came.

"I'll be right there; which building are you at?"

She told him and then bent over in pain.

⁂ ⁂ ⁂

The next morning Katie woke up to find herself in a hospital with her Mom and Tom standing nearby. They looked worried. She tried to sit up, but felt a little dizzy.

"I guess I really did get sick, didn't I?"

"You don't remember anything about the ride to the hospital?" Tom asked.

She shook her head, remembering only the pains.

"But you're fine now," Mom said. "The doctors just want you to rest today and then you can come home."

Mom and Tom looked at each other. Tom nodded his head.

"What's the matter?" Katie asked, noticing the look between them.

Mom reached over and took Katie's hand. "We'll talk more as soon as Dan gets here, which should be soon."

"Dan? Ah, Mom, that's not a good idea." She could feel tears again. Would they never stop? "No, I don't want him here."

"But Katie, why not? You're going to get married soon. He needs to be here." Her Mom looked at Tom again, as if she were trying to figure it all out.

How do I tell her, Katie thought. How do I tell her I just broke up with Dan? They expect me to get married. They're counting on it. But I have to tell them the truth.

Then the door opened, and Dan was there.

"Katie, I'm so sorry." He sat on the side of the bed and took her in his arms. It felt good, like he belonged there. Except he didn't. Then she thought of his words. Sorry. Sorry for what?

She broke away and looked at the three of them. "What's wrong?" No one said anything. And then she understood. "The baby?"

"The baby didn't make it, Katie," her mom whispered. "We're all just so sorry about this."

Katie looked at them in disbelief. So that's what the pains were all about. No baby. There was no baby any more. Why? What had happened? It didn't seem possible.

"Tom, let's go down to the cafeteria for a few minutes. I could use a Diet coke," Mom said.

After they left, Dan gave her another hug. "Let's forget what was said yesterday at the book store. You were just upset for some reason. But now? I feel terrible about the baby. Really I do. But there's time; we'll have lots of babies later. You know, this doesn't change anything for me, Katie. I love you. I still want us to get married. We could go to Bethel together. You could take classes there; they have more than seminary courses. And I've been saving money. Maybe we could get part time jobs. Katie, we could do it."

"But what about Angie?"

"Angie?" He frowned and looked honestly puzzled. "What has she got to do with this?"

"I thought you really wanted her. That you were just being nice because of the baby."

Dan kissed her cheek, then her lips. "No way," he said. "You're the one for me."

CHAPTER FOUR

FRANKLIN

> God is our refuge and strength, a very present help in trouble. Therefore we will not fear, though the earth should change and though the mountains slip into the heart of the sea.
>
> Psalm 46:1

Franklin Donovan glanced at his watch as he walked down the history hallway to his class room. It was quiet at this early hour – 6:30 a.m. Unusually early for him. With no one around, he could actually see the walls filled with posters about concerts, spring break, and the latest fund-raising drives. But he wanted to get out his golf folders and start thinking about his new golf team. Steve, the assistant principal, had given his approval for Franklin to coach a mini season this spring, along with the usual fall season for that sport. It was time to organize some practices, along with some competitions with a couple other schools who had golf at this time of year.

"It'll help us next fall," he had promised Steve last week in the assistant principal's office. "We can practice, play a couple of tournaments with East Springton across town, and get the kids motivated to work on their game this summer."

"It does seem like a good idea. But do you have time?" Steve had asked. "Remember, you're starting a new job as assistant principal of the freshman wing next fall."

Franklin had grinned. "Don't worry. I'd never forget that." He was really looking forward to his new job, even though he knew he'd miss the classroom in many ways. He had looked out the window at snowflakes falling. "I know it's snowing today. It doesn't even look like golfing weather. Good old unreliable March. But next week it could be sunny and seventy degrees outside, and we'll want to golf. And remember I should be getting a new assistant. My vote is for Nate in the business department. But, I know, I know, the position had to be posted and people interviewed before it's final. Hopefully that will be soon. This short season would be a good chance to get the new assistant on board and learn all about coaching."

"Good point," Steve had said, getting up from his desk. "And now I'd better run. Another meeting, you know."

Now, outside his room on this early Monday morning, Franklin took his keys out of his pocket, and was leaning forward about to unlock the door; but then he was slammed in the face by the door opening.

A boy rushed out the door, looked at Franklin in horror, and started running down the hallway toward the outside parking lot. Stunned, Franklin stood there, rooted to the spot. Seconds later, Franklin ran to the exit just in time to see the boy, wearing a black hooded sweatshirt with a red picture on the back, jump into a waiting car, an old beat up black sedan, and throw something into the back seat. Then the car squealed away. Franklin stood there, trying to take it all in. What had just happened? What was on that boy's sweatshirt? And what had he thrown in the back seat?

Confused and dazed, he rubbed his forehead where the door had hit him, and walked back to his room. Franklin turned on the lights and gasped. It was like looking at Emily's room all over again. When he reached his desk, which was empty, he knew for certain what that boy had tossed in the back of the car: his computer. He groaned. He had been in a hurry last night and had left it. Why had he done such a stupid thing?

Then he surveyed the room. A total mess. Desks over-turned, pencils and pens flung around, books all over, and a devil with a pitchfork drawn on a piece of paper on his desk. Maybe that was what was on the kid's sweatshirt. And what did it all mean?

He pounded his fist on the nearest desk, wishing he could pound that kid's face instead. The biggest problem was the computer; he couldn't live without it. Luckily, he thought, he always backed up everything and kept it in a locked file cabinet. But still he'd have to buy another computer and set up everything all over again. He immediately decided to never, never, leave his computer at school again. Nothing like learning the hard way.

After reporting the mess to Steve, he tracked down Ralph to get his help to clean his room.

"I'll be down as soon as I can," Ralph said.

"Uh, Ralph, this really is an emergency," Franklin said.

"I said I'd be down," Ralph said in a belligerent voice. "Gosh, there's always an emergency in this place."

Franklin looked at him in disbelief and clamped his mouth shut. It wouldn't do any good to argue or say anything more. But he hoped, again, that Jose would be back soon.

Franklin hurried to the library to see if he could hold the first hour class in there. Hopefully his room would be okay by second hour, that is if Ralph would get off his behind. Then he bought a coffee and donut in the cafeteria and took it to the teacher's lounge. He needed to sit, and think, and process what had just happened.

Pat, from journalism, walked in soon after he sat down. "Okay, spill your guts," she said.

Startled, Franklin looked over at her as he munched on a big bite of an apple fritter.

"What makes you think I've got something to spill," he finally said, swallowing as much as he could, and scooping up the crumbs in his hand.

"You told me, after Christmas, that you were giving up donuts."

"So? Maybe I just changed my mind."

"Or maybe something is wrong," Pat said. She raised her eyebrows and sat down opposite him. She knew him too well; they had been friends since his first days as a teacher there.

Franklin took another bite and looked around the room. Several other teachers were sipping coffee and looking at their cell phones. No one seemed interested in his problems. "There are just no secrets around here," Franklin complained about Pat's comments. "All right, all right. It was my turn to come into a ransacked room this morning."

At this announcement, a couple of other teachers turned around. "Not again," one said, shaking his head in disbelief.

Pat turned serious. "Oh, Franklin how awful. Was anything missing?"

"Just my computer."

"Wow. Not good."

"So now Ralph is cleaning my room, and he's not happy about it by the way, and I have to take my classes to the library."

"Good luck with Ralph," Pat said. "Seems like he complains all the time, and he's slow. Sure wish Jose would come back soon."

Franklin nodded his agreement as he finished the donut and sipped his coffee.

"Maybe they caught the kid on video. Have you checked?" Pat asked.

"Oh, right," Franklin said. "Thanks for the reminder. I almost forgot that Steve had a new security camera put in after the mess in Emily's room." He rose quickly, stuffed trash in the waste basket, and hurried off to the office; then he had to get to first hour in the library.

❋ ❋ ❋

Unfortunately it was lunch time before Franklin's room was cleaned up. It annoyed him that Ralph was so slow. He was sure Jose could have done it in half the time. He had almost lost his cool when he checked on his room after second hour. It was only about half done. And Ralph was lounging at a desk, talking on his cell phone.

"So, Ralph, any idea when I can bring the kids back?"

"As soon as I get done," Ralph had replied.

"But Ralph, the library won't be available much longer."

"It'll get done, I said."

Franklin had to mentally stuff his fist in his mouth to keep himself from a nasty comment.

"How about one more hour in here," Franklin had asked Libby, the librarian. "I'm hoping Ralph will have my room ready by lunch."

Libby raised her eyebrows but nodded her okay. "Luckily we're slow this week; teachers aren't into research right now I guess. After lunch, though . . ."

Franklin interrupted her. "I'll be back in my room no matter what." Even if I have to kick Ralph out, he thought. Then he flashed her a big smile and went to the other side of the library to talk to his students about what they'd be doing for the hour. This was an American history class, and he had assigned each one a Civil War general to write about. He was certain they'd appreciate the extra library time for research

Halfway through the class, Steve showed up, although Franklin didn't see him at first. Franklin was in a corner, grading papers when Steve sat down opposite him at the small table.

"Good class," Steve remarked. "The ones I talked to seemed to be getting into the assignment. Always a good sign."

Franklin smiled. It was a good day when your assistant principal had something positive to say about your class. Of course his biggest trouble maker, Adam, was absent that day; otherwise things could have looked a lot different.

"Thank goodness for that video," Steve said. "We could see very clearly who it was." He stopped as if to build the suspense. "Marco. Jose's son," Steve said when Franklin didn't say anything. "Also he's in Emily's fifth hour. I take it you don't know him?"

"No. Never actually met him. But why," Franklin wondered out loud. "Usually you think of an outsider, a non-student, doing something like this."

"I had to report this to the police, of course," Steve said. "It was a break-in and robbery. Could you come to my office for a few minutes after school? Louie from the police department will be there; I'll ask Emily also. Maybe together we can figure out what's going on with Marco. I hate to bother Jose while he's in Mexico if I don't have to, and I understand his wife doesn't speak English very well."

"Sure thing. See you later," Franklin said.

❋ ❋ ❋

After school Franklin stopped in Emily's room. "Did Steve tell you the news?"

Emily nodded. "It's Marco, who was absent today by the way. I guess I'm not surprised. He seems like such an angry young man." She grabbed her handbag and together they walked to Steve's office.

Franklin was surprised to see Marco there, along with Louie. Had they arrested him already? They were seated along the wall. Marco seemed to be carefully studying the color of his shoes. At Steve's nod, Franklin closed the office door and he and Emily sat down. He remembered Marco now; he had probably seen him somewhere in the hallways, although he had never had him in class. Most of his students were juniors, while Marco was still a sophomore.

"So, Mrs. Sanderson and Mr. Donovan," Steve began, "you can see that the police found Marco this afternoon. He and a friend were hanging out at the 7-Eleven near Marco's house. Your computer, Mr. Donovan, was in the back seat, apparently unharmed. You'll have to check it out, of course."

Franklin nodded and wondered what all this meant. First of all, he was happy that they had found the computer. That was a relief, as long as nothing had been damaged. But what about Marco? What would happen to him? And what about the other kid, the one driving the car? The room was quiet. Steve nodded to Louie.

"My name is Officer Androtti," he told them. "I found Marco, and he admitted to his part in the two break-ins. The other young man was not as forth-coming. He has denied everything, and since he's been involved in many other incidents, his case will be treated separately."

Franklin looked at Emily, who was frowning at Marco. He wondered how Marco was in class. Did he have a decent attitude, or was he a trouble-maker? Would they be asked to not press charges? Would Marco get no punishment?

Officer Androtti continued. "Marco hasn't been in trouble before; his grades are also satisfactory. We've talked to his father, who is in Mexico, as you know. He'll be home soon, right after the funeral of his mother."

Franklin noticed Marco's flinch at this news. Was this the first he'd heard of the death of his grandmother? Under the circumstances, had he had any kind of relationship with his grandmother? How sad to think of that possibility. What kind of world do we live in, he asked himself for the hundredth time, where families are separated because of borders. In spite of himself, he found that he felt sorry for Marco. He had missed out on an important family relationship.

"In the meantime, the police department is willing to try a lenient approach, if the principal and teachers agree." Then the officer outlined a plan for community service hours and a firm curfew for Marco for the next six months. "Any comments at this point?"

"Yes," Emily replied. "Three things. One, I agree with your lenient approach." She glanced at Franklin. "Of course I can't speak for Mr. Donovan. Two, I'd like to hear some words from Marco, right now. How does he feel about this situation, for example? Is he sorry for the two messes he's made? Three, I think Marco should have to write something. A letter, perhaps. Or an essay about this whole situation."

Interesting ideas, Franklin thought. Leave it to an English teacher! He looked at Steve and Louie, who were nodding their heads in agreement.

Louie spoke first. "Marco, I think it would give more strength to your leniency case if you did as Mrs. Sanderson asks."

Marco looked up at the policeman, probably thinking he really had no choice, Franklin thought. Which he didn't, actually. Marco was just lucky Louie was a compassionate policeman.

Marco looked at the two teachers. "I didn't mean anything personal. It's just that I get so angry. It's all so unfair."

"What exactly is so unfair, and what would you change if you could?" Franklin asked.

"My Mom . . ." Marco began. "She's afraid all the time. She cries a lot. She misses her family. She wants to see them, but she knows if she goes back to Mexico, well, maybe she'll never get back."

Louie stood up abruptly. "Marco, it would be best if I left now. I'll be in touch about the community service." With that, he turned and left the office.

Franklin looked at Steve. Was Louie thinking he'd have to report Marco's Mom if he heard any more? Had Marco said too much already? He could see that Steve was thinking the same thing. Steve gave Franklin a knowing look and nodded slightly. The room was quiet. Give Marco a little time, Franklin thought. He seemed to know what he should be saying. Might he even apologize?

Marco cleared his throat. "I'm sorry," he mumbled with his head down.

"We appreciate the apology," Steve finally said. "And we do understand the predicament that your family is in. That doesn't make it right, of course, to do what you did. That kind of thing never solves anything."

Franklin noticed that Marco's demeanor changed a bit. He was listening to Steve; his assistant principal was being kind and fair, he seemed to be thinking, from Franklin's point of view.

Steve went on. "If you do the community service hours and write Mrs. Sanderson a page about the incident, we'll let you back in school after a two day suspension. That kind of consequence would happen to anyone, by the way. So, would you agree to that?"

Marco nodded.

"Okay, we'll see you back in school Thursday morning. Be sure to give your writing to Mrs. Sanderson that day."

⁂ ⁂ ⁂

Half an hour later, Franklin tapped on Emily's classroom door and peered in. She was sitting at her desk with a stack of papers in front of her. "Maybe, if you took a break for a Coke, you'd feel more like attacking those essays," Franklin said, grinning.

Emily smiled back. "Great idea. Shall we stop at the Cardinal Café? Then I'll finish these up at home."

"Meet you there," Franklin said.

Emily filled her briefcase and was putting on her jacket when Ralph came in.

"Leaving on time today?" he asked. "Maybe now I can get home on time for dinner."

Emily couldn't believe what he had just said. He was so disrespectful. She zipped up her jacket and debated. Should she say something or just let it go. Just shut up, she told herself. With any luck at all he wouldn't be around that much longer. But it was hard.

Ten minutes later they were sipping sodas in the second booth from the door in the café.

"So what do you think?" Franklin asked. "Will Marco straighten out and get his act together?"

"I sure hope so. It seems like we're trying to help all we can."

"Are we being too nice? "Franklin asked. Then he answered his own question. "No, everyone deserves a second chance." Then he had a brilliant idea, or so it seemed to him. "What if I could get him interested in golf? That would help keep him busy and occupied. Maybe he has too much time on his hands to think about his family's problems."

Emily gave a thumbs up. "Terrific idea. Let's work on that."

CHAPTER FIVE

EMILY

Do not withhold good from those to whom it is due, when it is in your power to do it.
Do not devise harm against your neighbor, while he lives securely beside you.

Proverbs 3:27 and 29

There are times when I wish I could do so much to help other people. Like Jose's family. They're good people, really. Well, his wife did enter the country illegally a long time ago. Jose told me once that his wife, Maria, had come as a young teenager because she couldn't find any work in Mexico. She somehow got to Michigan, met Jose, and they married about sixteen years ago. She had thought she'd be safe, married to an American citizen. Somehow it hasn't worked out to keep her safe. Like new government rules. So now she is resigned to the fact that she can't go home again; if she did, she might never be able to return.

The door to Emily's classroom stood open. No surprise. Ralph must be in there cleaning. It was 4:00. Most of the students were long gone, having scurried away at the 2:45 bell.

Emily had been in a meeting with Pat, the other sophomore class adviser. They had one more event to work on – the proposed annual Spring Fling Barefoot Rock Dance in the cafeteria. An odd name for a dance, for sure, but one the sophomore committee had adopted after they overheard one of the older teachers mention the old sock hops of the 50s.

"How about barefoot night," Spence, the class representative, had asked. "It would be something different, even get the kids excited about Spring break in three weeks."

Pat and Emily had looked at each other, shrugged their shoulders together, and agreed to check it out with the assistant principal. "Seems like it would work," Emily had sad.

She left the meeting, then decided to get a stack of papers to grade before going to her car. After coming down the hall to her room, she heard voices inside, instead of a vacuum cleaner. She felt compelled to stop outside the door and listen.

"Will Jose be back soon?" asked one of the other custodians. Emily thought it might be George, who usually worked in the office and lounge area.

"Yeah, I guess so. Maybe another week," Ralph said. "Unless I decide to tell somebody what I found out."

Emily perked up her ears. What could Ralph be talking about? He knew something about Jose?

"What do you mean? Jose has been here a long time. I've never seen him do anything wrong."

"Well, maybe. Or maybe not. Or maybe it's about his wife, not him."

George waited, then said, "So what's going on?"

"I found a folder on that assistant principal's desk the other night."

"What were you doing in there?" George asked. "That's not your usual territory."

"Yeah, I know. Just thought I'd look around a little. There's no crime against that, is there?"

"Depends. So what did you find?"

Ralph laughed. "Good old Jose's family isn't all it's cracked up to be. His wife has problems."

"We all do," George said. "I take it you opened that file. Not too smart if you ask me. What if someone had seen you?"

"Well, no one did. And yes I did open it. You know how I've been wishing I could have a permanent job here? Well, I may have found a way to get it." Ralph paused, as if to build up the suspense. "Jose's wife is here illegally. That's what I found out. And I'm thinking someone else should know. Like the police."

Silence. Had that shocked George? Or had he known? Anyway it shocked Emily. Jose had told her all about his wife in confidence, but she hated the thought that Ralph had found out, and in such a way.

"Ralph, be careful. She's been here for years and years. You could ruin everything for that family. Just like you're ruining Sam's family."

"Sam? That loser in the freshman wing? He's the one who goofed up his life when he decided to steal from the school safe. Luckily I saw him. He and Nate help me with spending money."

"Nate? Another person you're blackmailing?"

"You know, some people just shouldn't get too cozy with women in Phys. Ed."

"Ralph, can't you be nice to anyone? They could all lose their jobs thanks to you."

"So? And do I care? I'm the one who needs a job. Jose's family should just go back to Mexico, where they belong. Leave the jobs for us 'real' Americans. And Sam and Nate? Who cares about them? They'll get another job."

Emily couldn't believe what she was hearing. Ralph sounded so callous, so hard and uncaring. For some reason she hadn't liked Ralph from the beginning. He had always seemed sneaky, even sinister. This seemed to confirm her worst suspicions. But what could she do? Anything? And what about Nate? Should she tell Franklin he could be in trouble?

Leave. Like now, she quickly decided. She turned around and headed toward Franklin's room. Was he around this late? It didn't matter; it would get her away from her room for a few minutes.

She turned the corner to Franklin's hallway and almost ran into him.

"I was wondering if I'd see you before you left," Franklin laughed. "Apparently you had the same thought." Then he took a good look at her. "You look pale. Is something wrong?"

Emily nodded, but she didn't want to talk just then.

"Should we go to the ice cream shop and talk?" Franklin asked.

"Good idea." Ice cream could solve lots of problems. "Let's walk to my room first so I can pick up some papers." Maybe Ralph would be gone by now. The last thing she needed was to run into him. Which they didn't. She could hear him cleaning the room next door.

❋ ❋ ❋

A few minutes later they were seated at a booth at Casey's Ice Cream Shoppe, which was just a few minutes away from the high school.

"So how are you doing?" Franklin asked after Tina, their high school server, had dropped off their strawberry and vanilla milk shakes. "This ice cream is a sure cure for all problems I've been told."

Emily glanced around before she spoke. The nearest customer was two booths away, but she kept her voice low anyway. "Right. Maybe. Maybe your problems. Maybe mine. But it's going to take a lot more for Jose and his wife." Then she told him what she had overheard in the hallway.

"Oh boy," Franklin said when she finished. "How awful for Jose. This isn't good. Seems like an impossible situation."

They sipped their milk shakes quietly for a few minutes, each deep in thought.

"You know," Emily said finally. "I think Louie, the policeman who was here with Marco, may know the family situation already. Or at least suspect."

"I think you're right," Franklin said. "I remember he left Steve's office quickly when Marco started talking about his Mom."

"Do you think it would help to talk to Steve and Louie right away, before Ralph decides to squeal?"

"I do." Franklin reached in his pocket for his phone. "I'll text Steve now and ask if we can see him before school tomorrow for a few minutes."

"And speaking of Marco, did he ever write that essay?"

"He did. Just read it last night." Emily stopped, sipping more of her milk shake. "I made copies for you and Steve."

"So what did you think?"

"Franklin, it actually blew me away." She stopped, feeling a tear in her eye. She cleared her throat. "It was good. Very good. Honest, remorseful, and yet angry at the same time. His mother's fears of ever going back to Mexico hurt him, and he wishes he could change the system, the unfairness of it all."

"You know, maybe it's kids like him who will change things one day. I'm sure there are many others in his situation."

Emily nodded, still feeling choked up as she remembered Marco's writing. She had talked to him for a few minutes after class that day, telling him it was exactly what she had in mind when she thought of the assignment, and told him it was a great piece of writing. He had seemed pleased. Even thanked her for listening to him.

"Have you thought any more about golf for him," Emily asked.

"Thanks for reminding me." Franklin wrote himself a short note on a napkin and shoved it in his pocket. "I'll get right on it, maybe even tomorrow."

"There's one more thing." Then she told him about hearing that Ralph is getting money from Sam every month, in exchange for not telling anyone about Sam getting in the school safe, and about Nate's interest in a teacher in Phys. Ed.

"Nate? Oh no," Franklin groaned. "I thought I had a sure thing in getting him as a golf assistant. Now I wonder." He looked around the room, thinking. "Lots to tell Steve I guess."

Then Franklin reached across the table for her hands. "Now, on another subject," he said, fingering her diamond engagement ring.

And then she knew what he wanted to talk about. "So you're wondering when I'm going to bake more chocolate chip cookies?"

"Well, cookies are always good, of course."

"Maybe you want an invitation to the sophomore Barefoot Rock Dance in three weeks?"

"Barefoot?" Franklin looked aghast. "You're kidding, right?"

"Not really. The kids think it'll be fun."

"I suppose it would be okay, especially if we old people are allowed to wear shoes." He paused and smiled. "Actually I'm thinking of a June wedding dance. What do you think? It's time to set a date, don't you agree?"

Emily smiled and nodded. He looked so excited about setting a date. He really wanted this. And yes, she did, too. Of course they needed to pin down a date. What had been her problem? Had she wondered about Franklin's feelings? The last thing she ever wanted was to make him feel as if he were being lassoed into something. Clearly, that wasn't the case. He wanted this marriage also.

"Get out that little calendar you keep in your purse."

She did, and handed it over to him. "I see we get out of school on June 9," he said. "I suggest Saturday the 24th of June. What say you?"

"Great. Let's go for it." It was done. Three months to do a little planning. No more stewing about the subject. She loved him. Loved the way he wanted to pin down the date. She smiled at him and felt tears in her eyes. Tears of happiness.

CHAPTER SIX

TOM

This is My commandment, that you love one another, just as I have loved you. John 15:12

Tom drove himself to church that Sunday, after stowing his suitcase in the trunk. He needed to get back to Chicago by late afternoon, but wanted to stop at the hospital to see Jared before he left. Tom couldn't forget how angry Jared had been, and how he had wanted the Bible out of his room. He seemed to hate all Christians. He had tried to calm him down with cookies, Coke, putting the Bible out of the room, and generally talking and spending some time with him. He was hoping Jared was feeling better today.

His mom and Franklin had saved him a seat, so he slipped in before the music started. He gave his mom a pat on the hand and looked around the sanctuary. The pews were full, but he didn't know many people yet. His mom hadn't been going to church here all that long; in fact they had rarely gone to church when he was growing up. Once he left Chicago for good, he looked forward to making this church a habit every Sunday, and meeting other people. He could easily get from WMU to Springton most weekends.

The sermon that morning was on love and how we needed to love each other no matter what our differences are. One sentence stood out for him: show people who you are by your actions, instead of preaching at them. He needed to remember that as he tried to help people at the hospital.

After church, his mom talked him into having dinner with them. "I don't want to see you leaving here hungry," she said. He was grateful. He followed them to the Fireside Room. Much better than stopping for a quick hamburger later on. In fact this was one of his favorite places. He loved the big, cozy fireplace, the high ceilings, the outstanding service, and the great food.

"We've got something to tell you," Emily said as she, Franklin, and Tom ate their lunch. Tom had just taken a big bite of his steak sandwich, so he nodded his head. He figured they had finally set a wedding date, and he couldn't be happier. His mom and dad had been divorced for several years; Franklin had been in the picture for quite a while. He knew his mom could be lonely at times, even with stacks of papers to grade, even with him and Katie still in and out of the house. And he liked Franklin. He had even had him for a history class when he was in high school. One thing he liked was how respectful he was to him and Katie. He never seemed to mind having them around, or made them feel unwelcome when he came to the house. He always talked to them as if he really cared.

"So you're nodding," his mom noticed. "I suppose you've guessed."

Tom gave a thumbs-up and swallowed. "It couldn't possibly be a wedding, could it?"

"We just can't put anything past you, can we?" Emily looked at Franklin and smiled. "June 24. I hope you have no plans that day?"

Tom made a big show of consulting the calendar on his phone. "That should work," he finally said. Then he stood up to give them both a big hug. He was happy for them. They had been dating for quite a while. It was time.

❋ ❋ ❋

After lunch, Tom went back to the hospital to see Jared, first stopping at the cafeteria for chocolate chip cookies and a Coke, and headed down the hall to talk to Cheryl.

"Peace offering?" asked Cheryl when she looked up from her desk at the nurses' station.

"Just thought it might help," Tom said.

"Actually it might. He's so restless and so angry."

"Ah, I had been hoping he was feeling better. Any idea what his problem is, other than the robbery?"

'I think it's related to him being gay," Cheryl sad. "Apparently the robbers were also making fun of him for being gay, even as they robbed him. So they not only shot him, but also called him names."

"It's interesting that he talked to you," Tom said.

"Actually it's because of you. I think he trusts us a little more after your kindness to him."

"Boy, he sure does have some problems," Tom said. He picked up the cookies and Coke, continued down the hall to Jared's room, and knocked on his door. "Care for a short visit?" Tom asked as he entered the room.

Jared glanced at him briefly, then went back to watching the football game. "Suit yourself," he said.

Tom put the cookies and Coke on the small table that swung over the side of the bed. "Just in case they don't feed you enough in here," he said.

Jared grunted and reached for a cookie. His way of saying thanks, Tom realized. He sat down and watched the game with him.

"Is your shoulder any better?" Tom asked finally at the station break.

"Some," was all Jared said.

"Say, Jared, before I leave to go back to Chicago this afternoon, would you mind if I prayed for you, that your shoulder will heal?"

Jared looked up at him with a you've-got-to-be-kidding kind of face.

"Why would you want to do that? I'm gay. You Christians hate gays."

"Well, I don't, and besides I listen to Jesus. Jesus loved everyone," Tom said after a couple of minutes, wondering if there was a right way to handle this situation. Then he decided to just continue. He prayed a short prayer for Jared. "I'll be back next Saturday; if you're still here, I'll look in on you again. Hope you have a good week."

Jared nodded. Tom briefly touched his arm and then left. Had he done any good? Made him any less angry? He didn't know. He'd pray and leave it in God's hands. Maybe he'd find out next Saturday, that is if Jared were still here.

After leaving Jared's room, he stopped to report to Cheryl. "He seemed to like the cookies," Tom said. "At least he ate several while we watched the game, and I prayed for him."

"He'll miss you this week," Cheryl said.

"You did what?" another nurse, Samantha, said.

"Um… the cookies or the prayer?" Tom answered.

"Well, both. I mean, well, he's different. He's not like you I guess."

Tom looked at her, puzzled. "His being different doesn't really matter. We're taught to pray for anyone who's hurting."

"Well, okay. Just surprising."

"We're to love everyone," Tom said as he left the nurses' station. "See you next Saturday."

Sometimes, Tom thought as he left the hospital and started the drive to Chicago, he found it hard to understand some people. Like Samantha. Sure, most Christians believed that a gay lifestyle isn't right, but this wasn't the time or place for that kind of conversation. Showing love in the hospital. That was the thing to do.

❋ ❋ ❋

The next week in Chicago was a long one for Tom. His job, selling golf clubs, was getting boring, he realized. People either needed golf clubs or they didn't, and it wasn't all that hard. And then there was his dad, of course.

"But this is a great job," his dad had said as they ate lunch one day. "You make good money, and it's not stressful at all. How could you quit?"

Tom thought a minute before responding. He had to say it right. He had no intention of hurting his Dad's feelings. "You're right," Tom admitted. "It is a good job, and I appreciate your help in getting it for me." Tom stopped and looked at his Dad, who was busy chewing his steak. Was he even listening? Sometimes it seemed like he had such a short attention span. "But now I have a chance to go back to school and get a master's degree plus a teaching certificate. Plus, the hospital really needs me full time until next fall."

"But you could work here until then."

So he was listening. "True, Dad, but being around a hospital and helping patients is very important to me. And with that degree I can teach later and help people in a different way. Of course, I may still work in the hospital part time. That's how much I love it."

His Dad just frowned. And then said something totally unexpected.

He looked at Tom, then lowered his voice. "I'll miss you, son. We've had some good times living near each other. Now you'll be so far away."

"Thanks, Dad. We definitely have had some good times. But Springton isn't that far away."

They finished their lunch in silence. There didn't seem to be anything more to say.

They did agree, however, after lunch and paying the bill, that this could be Tom's last week. His dad didn't seem to think it was necessary for Tom to stick around if he'd rather be at the hospital, and his dad could talk to the personnel manager about it. Tom would check in with the manager also, but it was nice of his dad to want to help out.

CHAPTER SEVEN

KATIE

> The Lord is my shepherd, I shall not want. He makes me lie down in green pastures; He leads me beside still waters. He restores my soul; He guides me in the paths of righteousness for His name's sake.
> Psalm 23: 1-3

By the time the calendars flipped to April, Katie felt almost normal. No morning sickness any more. Not sick at all. Just an emptiness inside her. Would she ever be able to have a baby, she asked the doctor? He assured her that she would be fine, and that the chances of a healthy baby later would be good.

Dan was wonderful during her recovery, and kept reminding her of their plans to go to Mishawaka in the fall, find an apartment, and take classes at Bethel. They'd be married, and a whole new life was ahead of them.

After a couple of weeks of rest, with no school and no working, Katie found herself going a bit stir-crazy. It was time to do something. The next morning she slipped on clean jeans and a new red sweater, a gift from her Mom. ("It's always nice to look bright when life gets us down," she had said when she gave it to her.) She had decided to find out what her chances were of getting any credits this semester.

When she got to the junior college office to talk to the dean, she found that two of the four classes would have to end with incompletes. There was just too much to make up. The other two teachers thought she could make up the assignments so that she could pass with fairly decent grades. She was encouraged to talk to those two teachers right away to get the make-up work. This was good news, and would mean a few more credits toward her junior college degree. She hoped Bethel would transfer all the credits from junior college. Sometimes she wondered if she'd ever catch up to where Tom and Dan were; both of them were now going to be getting post grad degrees. Well, maybe not. Her goal was a four-year degree for now.

When Katie told her mom she wanted to work at the book store again, for just a few hours a week, her mom wasn't very happy. She worried about her health, her stamina. Tom was the one who came to her defense, saying it would be good for Katie to keep her mind off of her loss. Tom even offered to drive her back and forth to school and work for a couple of weeks. That seemed to relieve her mother's mind. Mothers certainly did worry a lot, Katie thought. Would she be like that one day? Would there be another chance for her?

⁂ ⁂ ⁂

"Thanks for the ride," Katie said as Tom dropped her off at the book store on that Monday in April. She felt a bit guilty having Tom drive out of his way to help her. Maybe just a couple days of this would be enough.

"No problem, little sister," he kidded her.

"See you later."

When she walked in, Buddy was already there. "Hey, Katie. Dan wants you to be at the register today, and I'll shelve books."

"Sure," Katie replied, knowing that Dan was thinking of her and wanting her to have an easy first day back. He was so thoughtful. Working the register was okay, but fairly boring.

She was looking things over, making sure she knew what she was doing, when an older man walked through the door. It was unusual to see anyone over twenty-five in here, when all they sold were text books, shirts, sweatshirts, and goodies like chips and candy bars. He had gray hair, black glasses, and was wearing a black sweater that looked overly big on him, and was carrying a backpack.

After he wandered around a few minutes, she heard Buddy talking to him.

"Can I help you with anything?" Buddy asked the man.

"Well, I'm looking for a job. Just part time. Who would I talk to?"

"I'll see if Dan, the manager, is in the office."

After Buddy left, Katie kept an eye on him, for some reason. Something seemed 'off' about him, but she didn't know why. He could be her grandfather; why would he want a job in a college book store?

Just then a group of students walked in and seemed to head right over to the man, who shrugged off his backpack and put it on the floor.

Buddy went over and told the man that Dan could talk to him tomorrow if he wanted to come back.

"Uh, sure," the man said.

"Who should I say is coming?" Buddy asked.

"Ralph. But I'm not exactly sure about tomorrow. I'll see how it works out."

Buddy shrugged and went back to his book shelving.

Ralph watched Buddy walk away. Then he started talking to the group of guys.

Katie thought she heard Ralph say, "I don't charge much." Then he unzipped his backpack. What was going on, she thought. One of the students looked her way and said they should leave the store and talk outside. Wait, she thought. I remember him from American history. He always sat in the back, not saying much. Luke. That was it. Luke.

Shortly after they filed out, Angie came in. Her "good buddy". The one who knew just the right words to bring her down. At first it looked like Angie was going to avoid her as she walked down a side aisle looking for something. But then she came to the cash register with a book.

Angie swiped her credit card and then looked around as if to see who might be listening. "Sorry about the baby."

Katie didn't think she sounded very sorry, but she gave a small smile anyway as she put the book in a plastic bag.

"So do you go to church at all?"

Katie stopped and just looked at her. Church? Angie was now grilling her about church?

"It's not a hard question," Angie said in her haughty and snotty voice. "Just yes or no."

"Um, sure," Katie finally said. Well, she wasn't lying, not really. She had been to church with her Mom and Tom a few times.

"You know, Katie," Angie went on in the same "I-know-it-all" voice, "Dan will be going to Bethel next year."

"Yes, I'm aware of that," Katie said. That had been Dan's plan for some time. Of course she would know that. She'd be going to Bethel also. What was Angie's point?

"It's a Christian college. He wants to be a missionary."

"Yes, I know." Katie said cautiously. So what, she was thinking. What was Angie trying to say? Didn't she have anything better to do?

"So a missionary needs a spouse who will help him. Who loves God and is also a Christian. He shouldn't be marrying just anybody."

Katie opened her mouth in disbelief. Ah, that was Angie's point. She shouldn't marry Dan. She wasn't good enough, wasn't churchy enough.

Thankfully another student came up to the cash register, so Angie took her receipt and walked out. But not before she made one more comment. "Think about it," she called over her shoulder as she walked out the door.

That entire conversation put a cloud over Katie that day. She kept busy at the register, but apparently not busy enough, because Angie's words kept coming back to her. Mainly these: Dan needs a spouse who loves God and is a Christian.

Dan was busy all day, and she didn't see him, which was probably just as well. It was like she couldn't face him after hearing how inadequate she was.

Tom picked her up and kept the conversation going with talk of the patients he was helping. Some of the stories made her laugh, in spite of herself. She told him about Ralph and his odd behavior.

"I think I've heard Mom talk about a Ralph," Tom said. "A custodian at school. Probably not the same person, even though it's not common name."

Finally, about a block away from home, he asked her THE question and got more serious. "Is everything all right, Kate? You seem kind of quiet. Are you tired from your day in class and the book store? Is working too much right now?"

"Well, I guess I am tired," she said. Then, suddenly, a question came out of her mouth. "Do you think Dan and I are compatible?"

Tom glanced at her with concern. "It sure looks that way to me," he said. "It's obvious how much you two care about each other. And he was there for you in the hospital." He thought a minute. "What would make you ask that?"

"Well, he does go to church a lot, and wants to be a missionary."

"Ah… So that's something you don't have in common?"

"Well, it's just that I wonder if I really fit in with his life."

By this time Tom was pulling in the driveway. "I know Mom has dinner ready for us, so we better get right in. But if you want to talk about church sometime, like after dinner, I'm game."

Katie smiled, opened the door, and tried to put on a cloak of 'good attitude'. She didn't need to bring a cloud into the house. And she didn't know if she felt like talking more to Tom about it. What was the matter with her?

CHAPTER EIGHT

FRANKLIN

Bear one another's burdens, and thereby fulfill the law of Christ.
Galatians 6:2

A new commandment I give to you, that you love one another, even as I have loved you, that you also love one another.
John 14:34

Franklin was busy at his classroom desk grading quizzes on the Civil War when the door abruptly opened and Jose peered in. "Sorry, Mr. Donovan. I didn't mean to disturb you. But this is really late for you."

"You're right," Franklin said as he checked his watch. Sure enough – 5:00. "That's okay. You're just the incentive I need to get out of here."

Franklin shoved the quizzes into his briefcase, along with more quizzes for World History. Man, so much work to do. And it's all my fault, he thought, since I'm the one making all the assignments. As usual, there would be work tonight after he ate his frozen Lean Cuisine dinner all by himself. But not for long would he have lonely dinners, since he got Emily to pin down a wedding date. It would be nice to have someone to eat with every night.

"Say, Mr. Donovan, do you have a minute?"

"Absolutely." He sat down at his desk again and waved Jose over to the nearest desk. "Have a seat. We were all so sorry to hear about your mother."

Jose nodded his thanks. "I'm glad I was there, to see her before . . . If only my wife . . ."

Franklin was quiet, not sure what to say. Death was so hard on those left behind. "If there is anything we can do, let us know. Like time off? I know Steve would understand."

"Thanks. But I wanted to talk about Marco," Jose went on. "I really am thankful for all of you giving him a second chance. I don't know what that kid was thinking, breaking into your rooms. I didn't raise my kids to do things like that." Jose shook his head. "And stealing a computer for money? I guess he overheard his mother and I talking about finances one time. Never thought he'd stoop so low."

"No one is blaming you, Jose. We all do stupid things at one time or another, things that we shouldn't have done, and things we'll regret later." If others only knew, Franklin thought, how true that was for him. Probably for everyone. It was so easy to do the wrong thing. How often had he heard his pastor say something similar?

"Thanks, Mr. Donovan." Jose looked down, seemingly studying his hands. "I guess you know about my wife, and how we're worried about her being deported. She got busy with raising our kids and never got around to doing something about citizenship. We need to fix it now, though. She's been worrying about that a lot lately. I wish attorneys weren't so expensive."

Franklin nodded, not sure what to say at this point. He wished he could tell Jose to hurry up and do something before someone like Ralph told the police. But what could be done now, even with an attorney? The authorities seemed to be coming down harder and harder on illegal immigrants. Still, he decided to talk to Steve to see if there was any way the school district could do something to help Jose's wife.

Steve had been told about what Emily overheard Ralph telling the other custodian, about the blackmailing he was doing, and he was appalled. Since Ralph was a substitute custodian, Steve decided to request that Ralph go to an elementary school and not be at the high school in the future. But would that be enough to make Ralph forget Jose? Hard to tell. And besides, sometimes there was no choice as to where a substitute was sent.

"So, Jose, just to clarify a point. Is Marco an American citizen?" If he were to be on the golf team, it would be much better knowing that there were no citizenship issues.

"Yes; he was born here," said Jose. "And I am a citizen also. The school helped me a long time ago with the whole application process. I'm very thankful for that. If only my wife . . ."

Odd, Franklin thought. Jose became a citizen, but his wife did not. But since the school had once helped Jose with the process, maybe they could do the same for his wife. He wondered about Jose's wife. Sure, she had been busy raising the kids, but had she perhaps hoped to return to Mexico to live some day? Was she not as happy here in the states as Jose was?

Jose stood up as Franklin spoke again. "I had a thought about Marco. Our golf team could use some new recruits. Do you think he might be interested? We would teach him the game, by the way, and I'm sure we could find some used clubs for him."

"Maybe that's what he needs," Jose said. "Something to think about besides school work. I could tell him to come see you tomorrow. And thank you so much for showing an interest in Marco. That means a lot to me."

"You're so welcome. I'll enjoy helping him with my favorite sport. Now I'll get out of the way so you can do your job."

⁂ ⁂ ⁂

The next Monday morning Franklin made a stop at the cafeteria before heading to the teacher's lounge.

"Another stressful day already?"

Franklin looked up from his seat in the lounge to see Pat pointing at his donut. "I do believe you're back-sliding," she said.

"I know, I know," Franklin mumbled as he swallowed the last of the tasty chocolate donut and then took a swig of coffee. "Unlike you, I have a hard life trying to get juniors to understand the Civil War."

"I can understand," Pat nodded as she sat down opposite him with her coffee. "But you should be in my shoes. All I have to do is put out a school paper every week. I'm sure I have the hardest job, if you really want to know."

Emily came in just in time to hear Pat. "Is this a contest to see who works the hardest? If so, I need to speak my piece."

"I even worked Saturday morning," Franklin said.

"I thought you went golfing," Emily said.

"I was teaching Marco how to play. Trust me; that was work."

"Do you think he'll catch on?"

"Sure, with my expert coaching skills," Franklin smirked.

Emily laughed. "I'm just glad he took you up on your offer. I think he's been a little happier in class, too."

"Is that Jose's son?" Pat asked.

Both Franklin and Emily nodded.

"I always enjoy talking to Jose before I go home," Pat said. "I've heard a lot about Marco. He enjoys talking about his family. And Jose is also so much better than his substitute – Ralph."

"Yes. No contest," Franklin said. "Oh, is that the warning bell for first hour? We better hurry."

By the time Franklin quickly walked to his room, most of his students were waiting to get in.

"Sorry I'm late," Franklin said. He unlocked the door and turned on the lights. Students poured into the room as he put his briefcase on his desk chair and slipped off his jacket. "Let's talk about the Civil War assignment," he said as everyone was sitting down and getting settled.

"Any chance of getting more time in the library?" John called from the back row.

Franklin glanced at him and smiled. "We'll see." Then he went over to the closet to hang up his jacket. He opened the door, chuckling at the typical question, and came face to face with Ralph. Sitting on the floor. Franklin stood there, stunned. Ralph had a bloody face and a huge lump on his forehead. No, this couldn't be. Was he? Dead? Maybe, yes. Should he touch him? He felt his wrist. Nothing there.

Franklin stood there a minute, trying to comprehend what he was seeing, what he should do with a class full of students and a dead body in the closet. He closed the door quickly and turned around. Everyone was still talking. Apparently no one else had seen the gruesome sight. He had to think. Quickly. He'd take his class to the library and hope Libby wasn't all booked up with other classes. John had just asked for more time, as they had a paper due next week about the Civil War; each one had a general to write about. Yes, they could work on that. They'd be surprised that John had helped give them some extra time.

"Grab all your stuff, gang. Let's head to the library." The students looked up, surprised, but quickly followed him out of the room

"Hey John, good man! You need to speak up more often." Franklin heard someone complimenting John. Normally Franklin would turn around and kid around with them. Not now. This was no time for levity.

"Libby," Franklin said as soon as they all trooped into the library, "I've got a huge problem in my room. An emergency. Can I park the kids in here for the hour?"

Libby nodded and Franklin continued. "Ask John. He can tell you what the assignment is."

"Of course," Libby said, still looking puzzled. "Get to the office and I'll handle this."

Franklin, relieved, hurried to Steve's office. Thankfully Steve was there, alone.

"We've got a problem," he said as he closed the door and Steve looked up at him with a question on his face.

Franklin sat down. Where to start. This just couldn't be happening.

❋ ❋ ❋

An hour later, a quiet, normal Monday morning at the high school had turned into a three-ring circus, as Franklin would later describe it to Emily. The police had been called; crime scene investigators had taken over Franklin's room; Ralph had quietly been taken away out the back door; a sub had been called in for Franklin, and it was quickly decided that Emily also should be in on the discussions. She had heard about Sam and Nate being blackmailed, and how Ralph seemed to be a part of all that. It was natural that Louie would want to talk to her also. So a sub had been called for her. Now, Franklin, Emily, and Steve were huddled in Steve's office wondering how this had ever happened in their school.

"I was hoping Ralph wouldn't be subbing here anymore," Emily said as they sat down to discuss events.

"I know. I hoped for the same thing," Steve said. "But sometimes it can't be helped. Jose had a concert Friday night; his daughter was in the band at the middle school. So Ralph was subbing here. Apparently no one else was available."

"So he was killed Friday night?" Franklin wondered.

"That's my guess," Steve said. "I'm sure the police will know the approximate time soon. And something else. There was a knife wound in the back of Ralph's neck."

"In the back of his neck?" Franklin asked. "I guess I only saw the front of him, propped against the wall."

Just then two policemen, including Louie, came in to talk to them.

Louie spoke first. "Is there a room we could use? I'm thinking of talking to at least the three of you, separately, and then others if other names come up."

Steve let them use the principal's office, as he was out of town for a couple of days.

Since the body was found in Franklin's room, he was the first to talk. After all three had had their chance to go to the principal's office, they came back to Steve's with Louie and the other policeman, Devin.

"Each one of you has told us some interesting things about Ralph. Let's keep all speculation in this room, without discussing it with others. Please! If you hear anything suspicious about Ralph, however, from any other faculty members, let us know right away. We'll also be checking Ralph's computer for other leads. They all nodded and the two policemen left.

Steve, Franklin, and Emily sat silently for a few minutes.

"Why my room?" Franklin finally said.

"The killer doesn't like you?" Emily suggested, half in jest.

"But I haven't had any problems with anyone. That I can think of. Well, there was Marco ransacking our rooms. But that issue seemed to be resolved I thought."

They all contemplated Marco. He was certainly upset about his mom. But a sixteen year old killer? Nah.

"Ralph was not an easy person to get along with, for sure. But it's hard to believe someone would hate him enough to actually kill," Emily said. "Oh, remember what I overheard about Ralph and Sam? And Nate also. Lots of blackmailing going on. Could they have gotten tired of giving Ralph money?"

"Well," Steve finally said. "I'll remind Louie. I told him what you shared about Sam and Nate. So, you two have substitutes, and the police will be in Franklin's room the entire day. I'm sorry, by the way, that it had to happen in your room."

"You had no control over that," Franklin said.

Steve nodded his head. "Yeah, I guess so."

He was silent a moment as Franklin pondered what Steve might mean by "I guess so."

Steve went on. "You might as well go home and rest. You'll both be bombarded with lots of questions tomorrow."

They agreed, and left a few minutes later.

"It's only noon," Emily said as they walked to their cars. "Come on over to my place and I'll fix us a sandwich. I may even have brownies if Tom hasn't eaten them all."

CHAPTER NINE

EMILY

Finally, be strong in the Lord and in the strength of His might. Put on the full armor of God, so that you will be able to stand firm against the schemes of the devil.

Ephesians 6:10-11

It's hard to believe what has happened at school lately. Marco breaking into classrooms, Jose going to Mexico to see his ill mother, Ralph causing trouble as he substituted for Jose, and then Ralph found in the closet of Franklin's room. Dead. Teachers and students couldn't stop talking about Ralph. Rumors were flying everywhere; everyone had his/her own theory of why he was killed. And the newspaper reporters were all over school the next day. It is hard for students and teachers alike to get anything accomplished.

Emily parked in her usual space near the side door of school, pulled her purse and bag out of the back seat, and started walking. Then she noticed it. A large sign outside of the entrance, announcing that only teachers were to be admitted through this door. Everyone else, including all students, were to enter via the main entrance. No reporters or visitors were allowed at all. And to stress the point, a policeman was standing outside the door.

Good, she thought. Yesterday had been absolute chaos. Voices buzzing about a dead body. Guesses about how he had died, and who had killed him. Reporters all over the building interviewing both teachers and students. Steve must have talked to his bosses so the school could get quieted down. The end of the school year was only weeks away, so it was important that classes get back to normal.

Emily showed the policeman her teacher I.D. and he opened the door. "Thanks for being here," she said as she entered. He smiled and tipped his hat.

Once inside it was a short walk to her room. The hallway was quiet, a big change from yesterday. She put her briefcase down and unlocked the door. Thankfully the room was just the way she had left it yesterday. No chaos, no desks over-turned, no books on the floor. All was normal. She breathed a sigh of relief as she shrugged out of her jacket, hung it in the closet, and sat down at her desk to review her plan book.

All was well. She knew what she was doing today. As usual. In her mind, there were few things worse than not being prepared. So she always was.

She looked at her watch. Plenty of time to walk to the office, grab her mail, then get a cup of tea.

"You and Franklin have exciting lives," Pat remarked as they both entered the office at the same time.

"If that's what you want to call it," Emily grimaced. "It was awful for Franklin, that's for sure."

They both got their mail and began walking to the cafeteria. "I know Ralph wasn't well-liked, but . . ." Emily shuddered. "It's so hard for me to imagine disliking someone enough to kill him."

Pat nodded. "And then to put him in Franklin's closet. What was that all about?"

"That's one of the big questions," Emily agreed. They each picked up their teas, paid for them, and started back to their rooms.

Emily decided to walk past Franklin's room to say good morning and almost ran into Nate opening Franklin's door, with a golf club in his hand. She followed him in, intending to just wave at Franklin.

"Hey, that's quite a weapon you've got there," Franklin said to Nate.

"Mainly on the golf course," Nate laughed. "Just thought I'd see if you're available for a round of golf some time."

Emily waved at Franklin, glanced at her watch, and quickly started down the hallway to her room. Odd conversation back there, she thought to herself. Both the guys saw the golf club as a weapon. I suppose it could actually hurt someone, she thought. Then she shrugged and got to her room just in time for the bell, and no tea was spilled!

At lunch time, all the teachers were still talking about Ralph. Ralph seemed to be universally disliked by this group of teachers, and probably by many others as well. Many shared stories of run-ins they had had with him. One teacher had another interesting fact. Their assistant principal, Steve, had a brother named Larry. Larry was the mayor of Springton. Apparently Larry and Ralph had gone to high school together, and had been involved in a problem with a student athlete who had died of a drug overdose.

Emily perked up her ears at that. Could that be why Steve didn't seem to like Ralph? Not that he had ever said anything. It was just a feeling she had.

"Have the police come up with any clues about the killer?" a science teacher questioned Frank as he was chewing on his ham sandwich.

"Not that I know of," replied Franklin. Unfortunately most of the questions had been directed at him all day, since Ralph had been found in Franklin's room. "Honestly," Franklin went on, "the police aren't confiding in me." That comment seemed to stop the questions.

One person, however, still wondered about Ralph being found in Franklin's closet. "It's so odd," said Florence, who was a math teacher, "that your closet was chosen."

"That it is," Franklin agreed. "It's still hard for me to open that door."

Finally, to Emily and Pat's relief, the talk turned to baseball scores. Emily sensed the relief in Franklin as he went back to eating his sandwich. She and Pat tried to talk about other things, like kidding him about going to the Barefoot dance.

"You do realize I'll have shoes on, don't you," he asked.

"We'd expect nothing less," Pat laughed.

Then Emily remembered Nate. "So are you two exchanging golf clubs? Or was Nate giving you a weapon in case something else happened in your room?" Emily chuckled sarcastically.

Franklin smiled. "It did sort of look like a weapon, didn't it?"

"You know," Emily began slowly. "I just thought of something."

"Go on," Pat said. "All thoughts are welcome here."

"Did I tell either of you about a conversation I over-heard, one involving Ralph and Sam?"

"Sure. You told me at the ice cream shop."

"Oh, right."

"But I think I need to remind Steve." Emily checked her watch as she gathered up her lunch remnants and stuffed them into her paper bag. "Franklin, tell Pat about Sam. See you later."

"Hey, Emily," Pat called. "I have next hour free. Shall I go to your room in case you're late?"

"Oh, Pat, thanks so much. Yes. Just in case."

As she quickly scurried out, Pat and Franklin looked at each other.

"Sam?" Pat asked.

"Custodian in the freshman wing."

"Ralph certainly got around," Pat said.

Franklin nodded. "Sam was being blackmailed by Ralph."

"Tune in tomorrow, I guess. Lots of mysteries in this school." Pat got up from the table, followed by Franklin.

⁂ ⁂ ⁂

Emily returned to her class about fifteen minutes into the hour. "Thanks so much, Pat. I owe you one."

Pat smiled and slipped out the door.

In this senior creative writing class, everyone was actually writing. Happy days!! Emily walked around the room peaking at the papers. They seemed to be totally engaged. Every paper had the word Ralph on it. She stopped at Ellie's desk and quietly asked her what Pat had assigned them.

"She told us to write a page imagining why someone would want to get rid of a custodian," Ellie whispered.

Emily smiled. Pat had good ideas.

"Finish your page in the next couple of minutes if you can," Emily told the class. "And then let's hear some of your ideas."

Many students seemed eager to share.

"Maybe Ralph saw something he wasn't supposed to see," one boy said. "Like two people arguing."

"When he cleaned rooms, it was late, when there weren't many people around. A perfect time to snoop and discover someone's secret."

"What if he saw another custodian sleeping on the job, and then squealed on him."

Near the end of the hour, Emily had them pass their papers to the front, complimenting them on their good detective work. "I think I'll show these to our assistant principal, if you don't mind. It might help him as he's thinking of this whole situation. You never know."

One student, Evan, waited until everyone had left before he spoke to Emily.

"Did you think of anything interesting to write?" Emily asked.

"Well," Evan hesitated. "I heard something odd one day, after my accounting class."

"And did you write about it?"

"Actually, no. I mean, I don't want to get anyone in trouble. It's probably nothing."

"Well, I don't want to push you, but we sure could use some clues," Emily said.

"Hm…," Evan said. "Well, a lady gym teacher was talking to Mr. Tompkins in accounting class one day. She said we won't have to give that stupid janitor any more money."

"Ah..," said Emily. Mr. Tompkins was Nate. "Was the gym teacher blonde, slim, and short?"

"Well, I guess so," Evan said. Then he scooted out the door.

Emily looked after him, puzzled. Did it mean anything? But there was no time to dwell on it. She'd see Steve later. Her sophomore honors class was coming in.

After the last class trooped out of the room, Emily went to the office to see Steve. He wasn't there, naturally. There were always many things to do as the kids were leaving.

"He'll be back in a few minutes I'm sure," Julie, his secretary said. "Out with the buses, you know."

"Of course. I forgot." Emily found a chair, deciding to rest and look at the other custodian papers from earlier today. Maybe it was silly to think that Steve would want to see them.

Hm… This one was interesting. One student suggested it was a mistake. Two people argued. One pushed the other. One fell down and hit his head. Maybe it really wasn't an actual murder.

Steve walked in a few minutes later. “Hey, Emily, how was your day?”

“Great. Just wanted to see you for a minute.”

“Sure. Come on in.”

Emily quickly explained Pat’s assignment and showed him the papers. “I had this crazy idea that maybe you’d want to see them. Some other ideas to consider, maybe. Also, one student, Evan, didn’t write about this, but he told me about it.” Then Emily told him about the conversation between Nate and the gym teacher. And don’t forget about Sam, she reminded him.

“Thanks. We could have some real clues here. At this point we need to consider all the angles.”

“Oh, one more thing. I just heard that you and the mayor are brothers and that Ralph and your brother went to high school at the same time.”

“Oh yeah, I do seem to remember that. Okay, I’d better get busy with this report.”

Emily nodded and walked back to her room. Interesting. She mentioned his brother and Ralph, and Steve didn’t seem to want to talk about it. Oh well.

After getting back to her room, she spent the next two hours with her plan book and all the papers she still had to grade. They never seemed to disappear.

Then Jose came in. “Hi, Mrs. S.,” he said, peeking in the room. “I’ll come back later when you’re gone.”

“I’ll just be another ten or fifteen minutes, Jose. At least you don’t growl at me like Ralph used to.”

Jose’s smile disappeared. “I just can’t believe what happened to him. And nobody really knew Ralph before he was hired to fill in for me. Makes me feel responsible, I guess.”

“Now, Jose, don’t go down that road,” Emily said. “You weren’t responsible for all the enemies he so quickly made.”

“You know,” Jose said, “I keep hearing more and more of those stories. It makes me wonder if he had any friends.”

Jose waved and closed the door. Emily finished grading the paper she had started and decided to call it a day.

❋ ❋ ❋

Later that evening, she, Tom, and Katie ate their Cobb salads and chatted.

"Katie, I'm so glad that you're feeling better. Are things okay in the book store, and with your classes?"

"I'm doing okay, Mom. You've got too many other things to think about; don't worry about me."

"Katie, weren't you telling me about an older guy in the book store the other day?" asked Tom. "And wasn't his name Ralph? I remember you said he looked out of place because of his age."

"You're right. And he told one of the students his name was Ralph, and that's how I knew. Said he didn't charge much. And that's all I heard."

Emily frowned. "He doesn't charge much? Any idea what he was talking about?"

Katie shook her head no. "I remember the student's name, though. Luke."

"Katie, we've got to tell Steve about this." Emily drank some water as she thought. "I think I'll call him tonight. Would you mind if Steve wanted to ask you a question?"

"Not a problem. I'm not sure if it'll help, but . . ."

Emily nodded. Steve and the police needed to know any detail at all, of that she was sure. At least that was true in all those cozy mysteries she read every summer.

CHAPTER TEN

TOM

The Lord has heard my supplication, the Lord receives my prayer. All my enemies will be ashamed and greatly dismayed. They shall turn back, they will suddenly be ashamed.

Psalm 6: 9-10

How blessed is he whose transgression is forgiven, whose sin is covered. How blessed is the man to whom the Lord does not impute iniquity, and in whose spirit there is no deceit!

Psalm 32: 1-2

Tom's day started early – 7:00 a.m. – much earlier than in his old job with the golf company. But he didn't mind, well not too much. He was getting used to it. On the plus side he loved working with patients, and also when he left at 4:00, there was still some day left for other activities. Like going to the gym. He had signed up for a membership and started working out several times a week. It felt good. Not to mention good for a bit of extra weight he had put on in Chicago.

It was 6:45, on a brisk and windy day in April, when he parked his car and rode the elevator to the third floor. He wondered what patients he'd be working with today. Jared, perhaps. He was almost well enough to go home. Tom knew Jared was anxious to get back to his job at Young's Sporting Goods. The manager there had promised to keep the job open for him; he had been so grateful that Jared had stopped a robbery.

"Anything going on today?" Tom asked Cheryl as he arrived at the nurse's station.

"Looks like Jared won't be going home until tomorrow," Cheryl said, looking up from her filing. "Another test, I guess. Jared isn't too happy. He keeps saying he's got to get back to work."

Tom frowned. "That's too bad. Sounds like another cookie and Coke day."

"You sure pay a lot of attention to him," Samantha commented. She too had been filing, but looked up at him. And in a critical way, Tom thought. She was rather nice-looking – short brown hair and a slim figure, but her attitude took it all away for him. She seemed so judgmental, he thought.

"Well, he did a pretty heroic thing when he stopped the robbery at the store," Tom said, wondering why he felt like he had to defend Jared. What was up with this girl? "And I've gotten to like him. You just have to get past his gruff exterior."

"And maybe the fact that he's gay?"

"When a person needs help, it doesn't matter if he's gay." End of subject. Time to move on.

Cheryl glanced at Tom and gave him a thumbs up. Samantha just went back to her filing.

"So before you see Jared, could you go to rooms 301 and 308 and wheel them down to surgery?" Cheryl asked.

"Sure thing," Tom said and quickly went his way. He really didn't want to hear any more from Samantha.

He peeked into Jared's room on the way to 301. "See you later," he called. "And for sure this afternoon; I'll bring more cookies and Cokes."

Jared waved, as if to say 'whatever'.

Tom thought he must be really disappointed to have to stay another day in the hospital.

The nurses kept him busy the rest of the morning wheeling patients around and calming a young man just out of surgery that morning. Cheryl had frantically paged him with a message to hurry to room 324. When he got there the young man, Aaron, was crying hysterically as a couple of nurses looked on helplessly.

Tom caught the eye of one of the nurses and waved her over to the door. "What kind of surgery," he asked.

"It's his leg," she said. "The doctor had to amputate, and it was a complete surprise. Before the surgery, the doctor had had no idea how bad it was."

"That's huge," Tom said. He couldn't even imagine what it would be like to be in this situation. To lose a leg? When you hadn't expected it? But he was sure it had been a last-resort measure for the doctor. How could he help? He sent God a quick prayer. He knew he couldn't do this alone.

"Okay, let's do this. I'll stay here a while. Would you close the blinds, turn off the lights, and leave us for a bit? Maybe I can get him calmed down. Oh, and tell Cheryl what I'm doing."

She nodded. A few minutes later Tom pulled up a chair beside Aaron and touched his hand. "Aaron, I know you've had a big shock, and I can't tell you how sorry I am. I'm going to sit here with you and maybe we can figure out some things."

Tom sat with him for the next hour, at times talking quietly and at times saying nothing. Aaron finally answered Tom's question about his family. They were living miles away in California, and knew nothing of the car accident. He seemed relieved that Tom could call them. He even agreed that Tom could pray for him. But he no doubt needed more help. He'd ask Cheryl to contact the doctor about sending a counselor up to Aaron's room.

By lunch time, Tom was ready to sit down and relax with a sandwich in the cafeteria. Before eating he sent up a prayer to God, thanking Him. He felt that Aaron had calmed down, and that had to be good. He had just taken a bite of his tuna sandwich when Samantha sat down with her tray.

"Mind if I join you?" she asked.

Tom nodded a yes, swallowed, and waved her to the chair. Oh no, was she about to ridicule him for his stance on gays? "Sure. And how has your morning been?"

"Fine. Busy." She unloaded her tray and sat down opposite him. "But Cheryl thinks I owe you an apology."

Tom put his sandwich down. An apology? That was interesting. "Look, if it's about Jared . . ." he began.

"It is. Cheryl says my attitude isn't right for my hospital work. I guess she's right. I need to keep my opinions to myself. It's just that I've had some things drilled into my head from my church, and my parents, and . . ."

"Well, I do understand somewhat. The Bible does talk about homosexuality. But Jesus also talks about love and compassion." He took another bite to give himself time to figure out what else he could say.

"That's a good point," Samantha said. "I think I forgot that."

He smiled. "Cheryl is right; actually she's pretty smart. We meet a lot of different people in a hospital. People we might not want as best friends outside of here. But they're people, and they have problems, and they need us to care no matter how we differ." He stopped, hoping he hadn't been too blunt.

Samantha nodded. They both ate their sandwiches in silence. Then Tom looked at his watch and stood up. "I'd better get those cookies for Jared. Thanks for talking to me, Samantha. We all have beliefs that need to be looked at from time to time."

"Thanks, Tom."

He bought the cookies and Coke, paid for them, and headed up to Jared's room. He opened the door and found him engrossed in an old NCIS show. "Shall I come back later?"

Jared turned off the TV. "No, it was just a re-run anyway. And besides, those cookies look more interesting."

"I guess it's been hard, having to stay another day," Tom said as he deposited the treats on the bedside table.

"Yeah. But it looks like tomorrow for sure. Thanks for the cookies. And for listening to me. You've been a friend."

After chatting a few more minutes, Tom shook hands with Jared. "Good luck. I'll look you up at the hardware store some time and see how you're doing."

At the nurses' station, Cheryl looked relieved to see him. "Oh good, you're back. Another problem. This time in 335. Her name is Kelly. The doctor is fixing her up after she had a botched abortion."

Tom blanched. An abortion? He thought of Katie, who was still getting over the trauma of a miscarriage.

"Tom, she's not doing well. One of the nurses told her she deserved what was happening to her, that God was punishing her."

"Samantha?" He had to ask, even though he didn't believe she'd stoop that low.

"Oh no, not her. I think she knows better now."

"I can't believe a nurse actually said that to Kelly." What was the matter with some staff people these days, he thought.

"The nurse has been reprimanded. But in the meantime, Kelly isn't doing well, physically or emotionally. She's even refusing to eat."

"Will she be all right?" Tom asked.

"Sure. No one has come to see her, though. She seems to be all alone. The doctor has sent for a counselor, but could you look in on her in the meantime?"

"Of course. I'm on my way." What could he say, Tom thought. He didn't like abortions, either. But saying it now, after the fact, wasn't something Kelly needed to hear. What she needed was a friend.

He made a quick detour to the cafeteria for more cookies and Coke. The women there would probably chuckle, as he was becoming quite a regular there.

On the way to see Kelly he raised another request and prayed to God, asking for wisdom to say something that would be comforting. He would put aside his own opinions on abortions; they didn't matter right now. What did matter was comforting a suffering human being.

When he got to her room, the door was open and Kelly was looking out the window.

"Mind if I come in for a minute?" Tom asked.

"I'm not in the mood," she said quietly."

"How about if I just drop off these cookies and a Coke?"

She looked at him in disbelief. "Why? I'm not a good person, you know."

He set the tray down on the bedside table and stood beside the bed, sending a quick S.O.S. to God. What do I say now?

"Sometimes I'm not a good person, either," he said quietly. "Actually, none of us are all that good."

He offered her a cookie. "Peanut butter or chocolate chip?"

"Peanut butter? Really? That's my very favorite."

"And this is regular Coke, but I can get you a Diet if you'd like that better."

"Regular is okay. Thanks."

"Um, Kelly, no one has the right to say to you what that nurse said this morning. I'm really sorry about that. She did something very wrong."

Kelly finished the cookie and nodded. "Thanks."

"God tells us we're not supposed to be the judge of others. We have no idea what God's plan is for any of us."

"But does He hate me now?"

"No way. God loves us. He may not like our decisions, but He loves us anyway, and He wants us to have compassion for others."

Just then Samantha came in the room. "Kelly, the doctor wants you to have another X-ray. Tom, would you mind helping me get her there?"

Together they helped Kelly in a wheel chair, and Tom wheeled her out the door.

"Tom," Samantha said. He turned and walked a few steps back as she whispered to him.

"I heard some of what you said to Kelly. It really made sense. Thanks for how you're helping people."

He nodded and took Kelly down the hall to X-ray.

A few minutes later he felt the vibration of his cell phone and noticed the call was from Franklin. Tom stopped by the cafeteria to call him back.

"Hey Tom," Franklin said as soon as he answered. "Sorry to bother you at work."

"No problem; I'm in-between patients just now. What's going on?"

"Any chance you could join me for a round on the golf course late this afternoon? I'm going with Nate from the business department, but I'm thinking a game with three of us would be good."

"Sure. That would work."

"I'm thinking of seeing if he'd be a good assistant golf coach with me next year, and I thought I'd check him out. But it might be less intimidating if there were three of us, if you know what I mean."

Tom laughed. "Of course; you know that my golf wouldn't intimidate anyone."

"You sell yourself short," Franklin said. "Anyway, you can help me make a decision about him."

"I can be home around 5:00. Will that work?"

"Perfect. I'll pick you up soon after that."

CHAPTER ELEVEN

KATIE

> And not only this, but we also exult in our tribulations, knowing that tribulation brings about perseverance; and perseverance, proven character, and proven character, hope; and hope does not disappoint, because the love of God has been poured out within our hearts through the Holy Spirit who was given to us.
>
> Romans 5:3-5

When Katie opened the heavy doors of the college building, she felt good. Refreshed. Relieved. It had been two weeks since sitting in her classes, and now she felt ready to tackle the two courses where she could make up assignments: American history and English. As long as the subject of babies never came up. She didn't know if she would ever get over losing that baby.

The two subjects she was taking now were exactly what Franklin and her mom taught. She knew they'd be happy to help her if needed, and that was comforting. But she hoped to do it mainly on her own.

Fortunately both classes met back to back on Monday, Wednesday, and Friday mornings. That left her time to study and work part time in the book store.

This Monday in April she had American history at 8:00. The professor had e-mailed her the assignment, which was to choose from a list of Civil War personalities and find little-known facts about him/her. She had chosen Lincoln, and was armed and ready to go.

The professor made several small groups of four, and everyone circled up their chairs to share ideas.

"This was interesting." Katie volunteered to speak first when the group was formed. "I had never heard that Lincoln hated to be called Abe. He didn't even like the name Abraham, wanting people to call him Lincoln."

"And did you know," another student, Terry, added, "that Lincoln told his body guard a day before the assassination that he had had a dream that he'd be assassinated. How weird is that."

They all nodded, and others in the group shared what they had found. All except one guy, Luke. He just gave an excuse of having to work last night. Katie looked at him curiously. Suddenly she remembered. This was one of the guys, she was sure, who had talked to Ralph that day in the book store.

As the class neared the end Katie wondered if she should say something to Luke. Like, were you and your friends buying drugs from Ralph? Did that go badly? Maybe you guys decided to get rid of Ralph. He's dead, you know.

Of course she didn't. But she did manage to leave the room as Luke did.

"Kind of interesting about Lincoln, don't you think?"

"Uh, sure. I guess so."

"I think I've seen you in the book store. I work there, you know."

He just nodded.

"I remember one day I saw you and your friends talking to Ralph, a custodian at the high school."

"Could be," he said quickly. "Gotta go." And with that he hurried off down the hallway.

Interesting, Katie thought. I should mention this to Mom. She knew her mom and Franklin were very concerned about Ralph's sudden death, especially since Franklin found him in the closet at school.

Katie decided to go outside for a few minutes before her English class. She found a bench under a tree and next to large bushes. She checked her phone for the time. Plenty of time to chill out and enjoy the warmer weather. But she was still glad she had worn jeans and a sweater.

As she looked up at a few white clouds, she heard voices. Mostly she heard Ralph's name.

"He always seemed kind of creepy," one said.

"And his prices were way too high."

"Right. I almost told him to shove it, but I didn't. If you need it, you need it."

"He's dead, you know."

"Yes, I know."

"You do?"

Katie sat perfectly still during this exchange, wondering where they were. Perhaps on the other side of these bushes. All of a sudden no voices. Where were they?

She looked down at her phone and then to her right. She could see the backs of Luke and his gang headed back inside. She waited a few minutes, then sauntered to English. She opened the door and saw Luke. This was creepy. Why did he have to be in two of her classes? As usual, he sat in the back. She chose a seat up front. She definitely had to talk to her mom about him.

In English there was more group work, but Luke was too far away to be part of hers. They were supposed to talk about a short story in their textbook. Thank goodness she had read it. As a group they were to talk in general about life's disappointments and relate them to the story. Could the story be helpful to them? Each group had fifteen minutes to talk; then each person had to start writing about how the stories related to their own experiences.

A girl named Amber started talking first. She had long dark hair, perfect make-up, and clothes from a high-end store. Certainly not Penny's. Everywhere she went, people were dressed so nicely. Maybe someday she'd be able to afford more? Who knew? Then she realized she needed to listen.

"This story can't teach me anything," Amber said. "I've never had disappointments like these people had."

Katie looked at her in disbelief. No disappointments? Ever? How could that be? Hm. Maybe wealthy people didn't have disappointments? What planet was she from? Others in the group tentatively started expressing what she herself was feeling.

"You know, I don't come from a really poor family like this one in the short story," Joel said. "But when I think about my parents and their divorce, and my little snotty brother, it's not hard to find disappointments."

"But what can we learn from the story?" Amber argued.

"Maybe just keep going?" Katie said slowly.

"And have patience when bad things happen?" Joel added.

Then the teacher had them start writing. "Just put anything down at first. Get that pen going across the paper." Katie tried it and found she had a lot to write. The words seemed to flow out of her pen. She could really get into this subject.

After class, on the way to the book store, Katie thought about disappointments. It was hard not to keep thinking after just writing about them. How could disappointments be avoided? Probably impossible. There was so much to be let down about. Things didn't always work out the way we expected. Wasn't that normal? It was what we did with them, she thought. Like the baby. Like wondering if Dan was The One. She could fret and stew about it forever. Be upset and cry all the time. But what good did it do? The story made her wonder about just moving on after a while. Figure things out. Have some patience, because bad things were a part of life.

She wondered what Tom and her Mom would say. No doubt something about God. But if God was there, why did He allow these things – like a baby dying. She sighed. Her Mom was sure to have some kind of answer.

When Katie walked into the bookstore a little later, she found another reason to be disappointed: Angie. Why was she here again? Well, okay, she was a student and this was a student bookstore. But still. Most students didn't exactly hang out here. Then she saw Angie head to Dan's office. Talk about disappointments. She hated to think of Angie no doubt flirting with Dan.

Katie quietly walked to the employee area to stow her bag and sweater in her locker. Then she talked to Buddy, who was manning the cash register. "Any idea what I should do today?" she asked. She had noticed that Dan's office door was now closed, so he must be busy. Talking to good old Angie, apparently.

Buddy smiled. "Lucky day! Your choice of cash register or shelving."

"How about shelving," she answered. Perhaps she could avoid Angie that way, or at least avoid her after she left Dan's office. She went to the store room and put a box of business books on the cart. Probably nothing Angie was interested in. She glanced around, but couldn't spot her yet. Still with Dan? She wondered what they were talking about. Or maybe she had left? Maybe this really was her lucky day.

The next twenty minutes she dusted shelves and moved books around to make room for the new ones. The store was busy that afternoon, and she answered several questions about where things were. Like did they sell copy paper, or Civil War fiction?

"Actually, we do have a small fiction section," she told one girl. "Not sure about the Civil War, though. But they're over there under the window." And as she pointed she saw Angie and Dan coming out of his office. She was clutching his arm and smiling and talking excitedly about something or other. Too far away to hear, and too noisy here also.

Katie kept shelving, along with reminding herself to put aside the jealousy. Maybe Dan and Angie were discussing church activities. She just couldn't go on feeling like this every time the two of them talked. She remembered the class discussion just a couple of hours ago. Move on. Have patience. Figure it out.

"Oh there you are! Busily working away." There was no mistaking Angie's high-pitched voice. Nauseatingly fakey-sweet.

Katie looked up and smiled, noticing Angie's cashmere sweater and expensive boots, and continued shelving. She'd never be able to look like that. Did she want to? Maybe. Anyway she said nothing. Actually she didn't trust herself to say anything.

"Dan and I were just talking about a possible Fourth of July party this summer, that is for people who go to our church youth group. It should be a great time."

Keep working, Katie told herself. Say nothing.

"Dan agreed to help me with the decorating. So nice of him, don't you think?"

Katie put the last book on the shelf and rolled the cart past Angie and down the hall to the storeroom, closing the door firmly behind her. She wanted to scream. Why couldn't Angie just leave her alone? Why couldn't she just accept that Dan and Katie were dating? She turned around and came face to face with Dan.

"Oh, I didn't realize you were here. I just need to get more books. I think it's Spanish-English dictionaries that I need."

Dan caught her arm as she turned to walk away. "How about dinner tonight? Maybe that new pizza place on Turner?"

She must have looked surprised.

"Or are you busy?" Dan asked.

"Oh, no. Sounds good," she finally managed to say. "I'll be done here at 5:00."

"Great. I'll pick you up at 6:00 and we can go get all fed up." He grinned. "We'll find a corner table and talk. Maybe decide a few things." He opened the door and walked out.

She looked after him and just stood there for a moment. Decide a few things. Hm… Hopefully that was a good idea?

When Katie got home from the bookstore that evening, she found her mom in the kitchen making peanut butter cookies. They smelled so good; they were hard to resist. So she popped one in her mouth. While she chewed she watched her mom happily rolling more dough between her hands and putting the circles on the baking sheet. It was obvious how much she enjoyed baking.

"There's a guy named Luke in two of my classes," she said as she swallowed. "Um, good."

"So is there something wrong with Luke?" her mom asked.

"He's one of the four I saw in the bookstore talking to Ralph last week. And I overheard him and his friends today as I ate my lunch outside. Apparently his prices were high, but they bought from him anyway. Of course they didn't say what they bought, but I think we can figure that out."

"Hmm…" said her mom. "Very interesting. I'll tell Steve tomorrow. The police may want to talk to you, though."

"That's okay," Katie said. "I can't believe they'd kill him, though."

"Maybe not," her mom said, sliding another batch of cookies into the oven. "I guess we never know when one little fact can help."

Katie glanced at her watch and ran to her room to change. "I won't be home for dinner," she called back to the kitchen. "Dan and I are going out."

"Sounds good," her mom yelled back.

CHAPTER TWELVE

FRANKLIN

But Peter and the apostles answered, "We must obey God rather than men." Acts 5:29

On the way to the golf course that Friday afternoon in early April, Franklin was feeling exceptionally contented. He had just talked to Emily, the woman he would be marrying in a few months. They had set a date in June to get married. He would be putting lonely nights behind him.

And he was doing something 'fatherly' by going golfing with her son. Franklin had no children, having never been married, so he was trying to get used to this new role. Of course he would never take the place of Tom's father, but he could still do some things with him. Tom was sitting beside him and they were chatting about the latest golf tournament on TV last weekend.

"I'm surprised you asked me to join you," Tom remarked. "I mean I'm just a beginner at this game, really."

"I enjoy playing with beginners," Franklin said, smiling. "Most of the guys in our high school golf club are relatively new at the game."

"How long have you played?" Tom asked.

"Actually since college. My roommate in the dorm was into golf, and talked me into trying." Franklin checked the next street sign as they drove, and made a right turn. "I remember being surprised at myself. The game was fun and challenging. I have no problem admitting I'm not the greatest, but I still love to try. I know enough about the game to help the students, and I love seeing them get excited about playing."

Franklin pulled up in front of a small ranch-style house and stopped. "Nate, in the business department at school, is joining us. Actually I'm interested in your opinion of him. He's a candidate for my golf assistant next year. And you're a good judge of character, I've observed." Franklin noticed that Tom looked surprised.

But all talk was stopped when Nate opened the front door of his house, grabbed the clubs on the porch, and hurried out to the car.

"Hi Nate. I'm sure we can squeeze one more set of clubs in here," Franklin said as he opened the trunk.

"Great. Three of us this evening?"

"Right," Franklin said. "This is Emily's son, Tom. He's working at the hospital until he goes back to school this fall."

"Good to meet you," Tom said, turning to the back seat as Nate climbed in.

"Same here. It's great to get away from school for a fun couple of hours," Nate remarked on their twenty minute trip to the golf course. "I appreciate the invitation, Franklin."

"You're welcome. And I agree about the need to get away from school for a while," Franklin said. "It was bad enough when my room got ransacked. But then I find Ralph in the closet. Horrible. Just horrible."

"Well, I guess we won't have Ralph causing more trouble around school," Nate said.

Franklin glanced over at Tom, who was frowning. Is he thinking what I'm thinking, Franklin wondered. Nate's comment seemed a bit odd. As if he were almost glad Ralph was dead. Then he shook his head as if to clear his vision. That wasn't being fair to Nate. He supposed there were many who wouldn't be sorry to see Ralph any more.

❋ ❋ ❋

Three hours later Franklin dropped Nate off at his house and then he and Tom went to Emily's house. She was at the kitchen table grading papers when they trooped in the back door.

"Hi guys. Who's the best golfer?" Emily teased.

"No contest, Mom." Tom opened the cupboard for a glass and walked to the refrigerator for some cold water. He took a couple of swallows before saying more. "Franklin here skunked both Nate and me."

"Nate too?" Emily asked. "I thought he'd be more up to your level, Franklin."

"He's rusty, that's all," Franklin said. He looked at Tom's glass. "Hey, Tom, since I'm an old man compared to you, could you find it in your heart to get me some water, too?"

"Anything for the elders in this house," Tom joked. "But speaking of Nate. His comment in the car was a bit odd." Tom got the water for Franklin and joined him and Emily at the table.

Emily looked at Franklin curiously.

"Well, I'm sure Nate only said what many of us are thinking. He just commented that Ralph wouldn't be around to cause any more troubles at school," he explained to Emily. "That's pretty much all he said about Ralph."

"Hm… It's interesting how many people had bad experiences with Ralph. So Nate literally didn't say anything more about the whole thing?"

"No, he didn't. He could have said something about how bad it must have been for me finding the body, or maybe speculated on who could have been so mad at Ralph. But no, nothing," Franklin said. Then, thinking it might be good to change the gruesome subject, he asked Emily about plans for the weekend. "Do you think we should go to the Cactus Grill? And bring a pen and notebook. We need to make some June plans, don't you think?"

Emily nodded. "Great idea. In the meantime, I've got a chicken casserole in the oven. Hope you guys are getting hungry."

⁂ ⁂ ⁂

Saturday night Franklin and Emily went to the Cactus Grill. On the way there Emily laughingly pulled out a small notebook from her handbag to show Franklin.

"Just doing as I was told," Emily said.

"That's good to know how obedient you are," Franklin smiled.

"Don't get used to it, Franklin."

Once they were seated at a small table near a window, they both ordered Diet Cokes and guacamole to eat with their chips. A few minutes later they were startled by a voice near them.

"So you like Mexican food also," Steve said as he stopped at their table.

"Absolutely," Franklin said as he offered Steve a chip.

"Oh no, thanks. I'm here with a friend." Steve glanced across the room and Franklin followed his head to see an attractive woman sitting alone.

"I'm glad you're getting out," Franklin said.

"Yes. It's time." Steve smiled at Emily. "I know you know all about that."

"True, unfortunately. I mean, divorce is hard, and getting on with life isn't easy, either."

"Just one thing," Steve said. "The police called today. Said they were checking out Ralph's computer. They found a file on Nate. Also a file on Sam. Ralph was a busy guy."

"Nate and also Sam?" Franklin looked puzzled. "Like them all being friends?"

"No. Like Nate sending money to Ralph every month for the past year. There was a file of dates and money given to Ralph. Same with Sam. Ralph was getting lots of money from those two."

Franklin looked at Emily. "Steve, this is all so hard to believe. Not to mention sickening. What could have been going on?"

Steve shrugged his shoulder. "I guess Ralph knew something about both of them, something they wouldn't want anyone else to know. The police were going to talk to Nate today, but apparently he's out of town."

"Oh, I remember Nate talking about going to a cousin's party this weekend, down in Indiana I think."

"So we agreed to have a meeting at school Monday after sixth hour, in my office. By then they should have also talked with Sam also. I'll keep you posted, especially since you've wanted Nate as your assistant golf coach." Steve waved and left.

Franklin looked at Emily in dismay. "This doesn't look good at all. Maybe he won't be my assistant coach after all?"

"You're assuming he did something wrong. Nate seems too laid-back to be considered a killer," Emily said. "Sam, too, for that matter. Who could have wanted to hurt Ralph so badly?"

"So many people were angry with him, or had problems with him," said Franklin. "But killing? It seems impossible. Yet it happened."

"Just had a thought," Emily said slowly. "What if it were unintentional?"

"As in an accident?" Franklin asked. "Well, there was the knife wound. But perhaps whoever did that hadn't intended the whole incident would go that far? This is getting complicated."

The waiter came to take their orders. "Shall we share the chicken enchiladas?" Franklin asked Emily.

"Perfect."

With that taken care of, Emily brought out her notebook. "I called the church," she said. "Pastor agreed to June 24, 4:00, in the sanctuary. I told him it would be a small group there. Let's figure out who we'd like with us that day."

Franklin smiled. Yes, this was really going to happen. He was a mighty lucky guy.

CHAPTER THIRTEEN

EMILY

Where there is no vision, the people are unrestrained, but happy is he who keeps the law. Proverbs 29:18

My soul has been rejected from peace; I have forgotten happiness." Lamentations 3:17

This whole business with Ralph has everyone at school wondering. How exactly did he die? Which one of his enemies could have killed him? And there seemed to be so many suspects. Every time I turn around I hear of someone else who hadn't liked him. And even hated him. I wonder if he had ever had a real friend. How unhappy he must have been. Perhaps that was at the root of his antagonistic behavior toward everyone.

It was a Monday morning in April, and Emily was at school early. She opened the door to her room, stowed her briefcase inside, and then scurried to the business department. Thanks to Pat talking to Nate, they now had some help with the business side of their sophomore class obligations. He had started helping this year, becoming like a business manager. It gave them more time to work with the kids. Now she was ready to unload more proceeds from the Barefoot dance.

"Mrs. Sanderson!" called one of the sophomores. "That dance was so much fun. And I even saw you barefoot!"

Emily smiled and waved at the girl's enthusiasm. Yes, it had turned out to be a good evening, and the kids had liked the idea of something different.

When she opened the business office door, one of the guys told her to have a seat over by the coffee pot, and that Nate was around somewhere. The coffee pot and a small table were tucked away in the corner near a small windowless room that was probably used for conferences with parents.

She poured herself a small cup and sat down to wait, thinking of what she'd be doing in class that day. If Nate didn't turn up soon, she'd have to get back to her room. There were some things she needed to write on the board about the assignments.

She opened her bag, found her phone, and began scrolling down Facebook. Nothing too important. Just more problems with one of the senators. All of a sudden she became aware of voices in the little office next to her. Was that Nate? She thought so, but she didn't recognize the woman's voice. She heard the word Ralph. Then a laugh. "At least I don't have to worry about him anymore," she heard Nate say. "Let's take a little trip with the money I'm saving."

A few minutes later the door opened and Emily looked busily down at her cell phone. Nate was by himself. Where was the girl? Another exit from the room?

"Hey Nate," she called as he started walking to his desk.

He turned around with a startled expression on his face. "Oh, hi Emily. Have you been waiting long?"

"No, just got here." She didn't want him to think she had heard anything.

She stood up, opened her purse, and pulled out the envelope full of cash. "Pat and I so appreciate your help. I think we did pretty well the other night at the dance. When you figure out our bills, let me know the results, okay?"

He nodded. She laid the envelope on his desk and hurried out. After what she had just heard, the last thing she wanted was some trivial talk right now. His comment about saving lots of money didn't sound good for him, though. But it was time to go - almost time for classes to start.

Emily decided to take a quick detour to Franklin's room before classes started. "You'll never believe what I just heard," she said as she opened his door. Then she saw Steve. "Oh, I'm so sorry. Didn't mean to interrupt," she said, backing out.

"That's okay," Steve said. "I was just telling Franklin about the police report on Ralph; come on in."

Emily came back in and closed the door. They must have come to a conclusion about the cause of death. "So do they know how he actually died?"

"Yeah. A knife in the neck."

"What?" Franklin said. "So it wasn't just the huge bump on his head?"

"Right," Steve said. "When we both saw him, we only saw the front of him. Makes me wonder. Did he have a fight and fall, hitting his head, and then someone finished him off with a knife?"

Emily looked at Steve, thinking that this whole thing was getting more and more complicated. There were so many people who were mad or disgusted or just had plain hatred for Ralph. How would they ever find the real killer?

She detected something else about Steve. He seemed a bit relieved to learn the real cause of death. Why? Or was that just her imagination? Her kids always said she over-analyzed everything.

"And I just overheard Nate talking," she started. Then suddenly the door opened again, and a group of students walked in. Emily looked at the clock on the wall. Good grief.

"Talk later, gentlemen," she said as she rushed out the door. Time to leave this mystery behind and concentrate on her job.

Emily had a chance to finish her conversation at lunch as she ate her usual yogurt and apple while Franklin and Pat ate sandwiches.

"So back to your room this morning," she said to Franklin. "I overheard something in the business office."

Both Pat and Franklin looked up, expectantly, from their sandwiches.

"I overheard Nate telling some girl that he'd have more money now that Ralph was gone, and that now they could take a little trip."

"So Ralph was blackmailing Nate, too?" Pat asked. "I'm feeling we're living in some kind of soap opera on TV."

"Oh, boy," Franklin said, clearly disturbed. "But I sure can't see him as a killer."

Both Emily and Pat nodded their agreement.

"Well," said Emily as she gathered up her trash and got ready to head back to her room, "On another subject. I'm going to get a mystery package in the mail soon, maybe today."

"Just tell me there's no dead body involved," Franklin said.

"Well, not directly. But it does involve my parents, who died last January you may remember."

"Of course I remember," Franklin said. "A hard time for your family."

Emily nodded. "So this package contains a journal that the new owners of my parents' house found."

"That was months ago. They're just now finding something?"

"Odd," Pat said. "Where was it hiding?"

"There was a closet in the extra bedroom, and apparently it was hidden back on a high shelf."

"That was nice of them to look you up and send it," Franklin observed.

A warning bell rang as all three stood up to go back to their rooms.

On the way to her fifth hour Creative Writing class, Emily was hit with an idea. This package could be the beginning of a writing prompt.

"Good afternoon," she called out to the class loudly as she closed the door. "Get out a fresh sheet of paper and a pen." She stood in front of her desk, glancing around to see if anyone was absent, and waited a moment for voices to be silenced.

"Okay, here's the set-up. Your grandparents died last year in Iowa. Their house was sold. Your parents sold or got rid of all the belongings. Now it's a year later. The new owners found a journal, written by your grandma, hidden on the top shelf of a closet. The new owners send it to you. How does this now affect your life, or does it?"

Emily waited a moment for that question to sink in. "Now write a two page scene with two people and their dialogue."

The students were quiet, looking thoughtful. "Let's write for twenty minutes and see where we are."

Emily sat at her desk, wondering also. She hoped the journal would have arrived by the time she got home. And would it have some surprises when she read it?

❋ ❋ ❋

After class, a couple of students stopped by Emily's desk to comment on the assignment.

"That journal gave me an idea," Nikki said as she put on her jacket.

"Oh yeah?" Emily asked. It was fun to see the students get into the writing.

"Yeah, a story idea. A mystery about a baby that Grandma had and gave up for adoption."

Emily looked thoughtful. "You know, that really is a good idea. I'll be assigning a story soon. Maybe you could use that."

Nikki smiled. She seemed pleased that her teacher could see some merit in her idea. Sometimes we all need a boost, Emily thought as Nikki waved and sailed out the door. We all need to hear something positive about what we do and think.

After the students left, Emily began straightening her desk, getting out her plan book, and thinking about tomorrow's classes.

There was a light knock on the door, and Pat came in holding a newspaper. "You'll never guess what's in today's paper," she said, laying a section on top of Emily's desk.

"A good cookie recipe?" Emily said, kiddingly.

"Hardly," Pat answered. "Ralph's obituary. Did you know that Ralph went to our very own Springton High twenty years ago?"

"I do remember that from the other day at lunch," Emily said.

"He was also a football player in high school."

"And so was our mayor about the same time. I remember the mayor talking about it in one of his speeches. He's related to Steve, you know," Emily said.

"I guess one of the teachers also mentioned that at lunch," Pat said. She folded the paper and started to leave.

"You know," Emily said, "Ralph seemed to love blackmailing people. Do you suppose he got to our Steve in some way?"

"I wonder," Pat said. "Probably a long shot, though. I can't see Steve letting someone blackmail him."

"You're probably right. But Ralph seemed to be everywhere causing trouble," Emily said. "A busy guy."

Pat left then, and looking at the clock, Emily decided get busy on plans for tomorrow. Then she needed to talk to Franklin about the news in that paper.

CHAPTER FOURTEEN

TOM

And He said to them . . . "Follow me, and I will make you fishers of men." Matthew 4:19

"Hey, Tom," someone yelled as Tom walked out of the hospital, headed to his car and then a relaxing evening of doing nothing. Nothing. His day had been long, with several patients needing extra care. He loved doing it. Loved the feeling of being needed. But now it was time to rest.

Then he realized it was his Dad's voice calling him. So he was here, in Springton, and not in Chicago? Oh, great. He turned and tried to find his happy smile. Of course he was always happy to see his Dad. But right now? And did Dad have an agenda, like trying to talk him back into the golf shop? Then he spotted him near the ramp to the parking lot. Tom trotted over to the car, reaching in to give his dad a half hug.

"This is a surprise," Tom said. "What brings you away from the big city?"

"Just this son of mine," Jack said. "I kind of miss not seeing him every day. So I left work early and decided to see what you and Katie were doing. Like maybe you'd have time for dinner?"

Tom nodded. Well, so much for a quiet evening. He wondered if Katie had plans with Dan. "Okay. Have you called Katie yet?"

"I did. She agreed to meet us before seeing Dan later tonight. How about Freddy's Chop House over on Fourth Street? She kind of wanted to do it right away, though. Would that work out for you?"

"Sure. I'll just send a text to Mom so she doesn't start cooking for us, and I'll meet you over there."

Ten minutes later all three of them were seated in front of the fireplace in the main room, drinking, of all things, plain water.

"Cokes and iced tea are just too expensive," his dad pronounced, looking at both of them, perhaps to gauge their reactions. "But I'll be glad to pick up the tab for the dinners," he added.

"Sure, Dad," Tom said without looking at Katie. He was afraid he'd start laughing. Their Dad had had this aversion to drinking anything but free water for quite a while, unlike their Mom who had to have her Diet Cokes. Oh well. It didn't matter. Just another way his Mom and Dad were so different from each other.

Dinner was good. Tom and his dad chowed down thick hamburgers while Katie just had a salad. Both Katie and Tom talked about their jobs, so everything was friendly. As they were leaving the restaurant, Jack surprised them with his next announcement. "I'm going to say good-bye at your Mom's house. I need to talk to all of you for a few minutes."

Tom looked at Katie and raised an eyebrow. This was unusual. He could not remember the last time his parents had ever talked civilly to each other. Theirs had not been a friendly divorce. He and Katie had been in their teens when it happened. It had been a hard time for everyone.

The caravan of three cars pulled up in front of Emily's house. Franklin was there, Tom noticed right away. This should be interesting, he thought. He opened the door and they all trooped in.

"Hey Mom," Tom called. "Dad is here and wants to talk."

"Uh, Katie and Tom, this actually concerns you also. Do you have a few minutes?" their dad asked.

They both nodded and then Emily walked in.

"I won't take up much of your time," Jack said as Emily gestured them to the couch and chairs. "It's about my Dad."

"Is he still in a nursing home?" Emily asked. "I hope he's doing all right."

Tom knew that his mother had always liked and respected Jack's parents. He was glad that they were being polite to each other.

"Yes, he is," Jack said. "I went to Florida to see him over Christmas. It seems he has some property up here in Michigan. I had forgotten all about it. Anyway I guess he's been going through all his papers trying to get organized for the end. So now he wants to sell the land, since he has no use for it."

Interesting, Tom thought. He had never heard about the property. Perhaps his grandparents had thought they'd build a house there one day.

Jack went on. "So, he'd like to give you and Katie the proceeds after the sale."

Tom looked at Katie in surprise. He certainly hadn't expected anything like this, but he didn't really need the money, since his former patient had left him a lot. But this could be just what Katie and Dan needed. Katie could use it for school. Maybe actually get that degree. In fact . . .

"Dad," Tom said. "I don't know if you remember or not. But I had a patient leave me money last year after he died. Could Katie have my share? She could finally finish college, and use it when she and Dan get married."

"Well, I guess that would be okay," Jack said.

"Oh, Tom," Katie started. Tom saw tears in her eyes. "Are you sure? "Oh my gosh, I can't believe all this." She got out of her chair and crossed the room to Tom and her Dad, giving hugs to both of them.

"Thank you, Jack," Emily said. "That was so generous of your father, and you've made our kids very happy. Please tell him how grateful everyone is."

And then Emily went on after a pause. "Tom and Katie, and Jack, would you mind if I share this news? Franklin is in the den watching television. Maybe I could ask him to come out?"

Tom looked at Katie, who shrugged, and then at his Dad, who was looking a bit irritated. "What do you think, Dad? After all, Mom is marrying Franklin this summer."

Jack stood up abruptly. "Sorry, but I've got to go."

He was almost at the door when Emily spoke. "Thanks again, Jack. This gift means a lot to all of us."

"I'm sure it does," Jack said, turning the knob and opening the door. "Now you can start a new life and not have to do anything for the kids." With that, he walked out and slammed the door.

Emily stood there, looking at the closed door. Tom walked over to her and put his arm around her shoulders.

"I'm sorry Dad had to say that," Tom said. "I know he can voice things without thinking through what he's saying."

"Thanks, Tom," Emily said. "I didn't mean to spoil the evening."

"Mom, this is not your fault."

"Well, I think I'll go tell Franklin anyway. And then should I get out some brownies and Cokes?"

"Great idea, and we'll help."

Tom and Katie went to the kitchen to get Cokes out while Emily walked down the hall to the den.

"Mom was trying not to cry," Tom said to Katie. "Her eyes looked full of tears."

"I don't understand," Katie said, looking for brownies in the cupboard. "Dad can be so nice at times. Why did he have to spoil it? Is it possible he's upset about Mom marrying again?"

"I don't know. We'll probably never really understand," Tom said. "We haven't walked in their shoes."

Then Emily walked in with Franklin. "Kids you do know I'll always be there for you, don't you? No matter what happens. Nothing, nothing will ever change that," Emily said.

They all hugged again.

Then Franklin spoke. "And before we chow down on those brownies, I also want to say something. You two are the most important people in your Mom's life. Nothing she and I do will ever change that. I'm not here to in any way take her away from you."

"Thanks, Franklin; you deserve the first brownie," Tom said. "Let's go sit by the fire and enjoy them."

Everyone was quiet as they ate brownies, sipped Cokes, and gazed at the fire. Tom thought about the upcoming marriage, and was happy for his Mom and Franklin. It had never even entered his mind that she would forget Katie and him. Why did his dad have to spoil things?

Then Franklin broke the quiet. "Did your package come today?" he asked Emily.

"No. Maybe tomorrow. Tom and Katie, did I tell you about the journal?"

They both shook their heads.

"It's coming from the people who bought my parents' house. They found a journal in one of the closets."

"Sounds interesting," Tom said. "Maybe you'll learn something new about your parents?"

"I had my Creative Writing class write about it. Lots of interesting ideas. Like finding out that the mother had really dropped out of high school. Or the mother once had a drug problem. Or the mother had a baby and gave it up for adoption."

"Or there could be no mystery at all," Tom said. "Just ordinary things going on."

"Stay tuned," Emily said, smiling.

CHAPTER FIFTEEN

KATIE

> Even though I walk through the valley of the shadow of death, I fear no evil, for You are with me; Your rod and Your staff they comfort me.
> Psalm 23:4

Katie and Dan walked through the large double doors of his church on Sunday, into the lobby, and everyone they passed called out to him. She looked up at Dan, noticing how he loved all the interaction with these people – both young and old. There were several tables near the walls where people could sign up for a special event or get a missionary newsletter. At one there was a visiting missionary from Peru talking about his work with the Quechua people. They lingered at that table; then Dan checked his watch and said they'd better get a seat in the sanctuary.

After they found a place near the middle, Katie sat down and looked around at the large cross on the wall, at the choir waiting to sing, and at the large oval windows along one side. She had been here a few times before with Dan, but somehow she felt a little nervous this time, and she couldn't have said why. Was it that she didn't really belong, that she was not part of this group that easily talked about Jesus? But this was Dan's group. And really, she would like to belong. But how? Why? Angie would say she had better belong if she was going to marry Dan. Tom and her mom would probably agree.

The woman at the piano started playing the prelude, and the room became quiet. Soon a leader stood up and invited the congregation to sing a couple of hymns. The choir sang alone next. It was all fine, and she dutifully followed along.

The pastor went to the front, gave a few announcements, and then indicated that communion was next. He encouraged only believers to take the cracker and juice cup. Katie looked at Dan, wondering. He patted her hand and whispered, "It's okay." Yet again she was an outsider. She should have stayed home in bed, maybe pretended to be getting the flu.

After passing up the crackers and cups, and hoping no one noticed, she listened to the pastor starting his sermon. She looked at the bulletin and noticed that the title was "I did it my way." Hmm… she thought. Wasn't there an old song with those words?

Twenty minutes later, Katie was surprised at how fast the time was passing. The pastor was a good speaker. He made sense, as if he were talking just to her. We want to run our own lives, he said. And Katie could relate. She didn't want others telling her what to do. He went on to say that sometimes Jesus interferes with our plans. He wants us to follow Him and listen to His ideas. Two other sentences stood out for her. We want a God we can control. And, we don't believe because we don't want to believe.

Wow, she thought. There was much to contemplate. She wondered what Tom would think. Maybe it was time she asked him some questions.

After church, Dan led her down the hall to a Sunday school class. There were twenty five or thirty young people their age talking, drinking coffee, and eating some yummy snacks from a side table. She saw Angie, of course. But she seemed too busy talking to the group around her to acknowledge Katie. That was okay, Katie thought; she saw enough of Angie in the book store.

"So you're Katie, right?" a girl said, coming up to pick up a brownie. "These are good; you'll love them. I'm Julie, by the way."

I might as well eat, Katie thought. The brownies seemed to be calling her name; so she started munching as Julie talked.

"I hear you work at the college book store. My boyfriend, Buddy, works there too."

Katie smiled and nodded. "Of course. A great guy."

"I hope you're not interested in him," Julie continued. "He's mine, and I don't share."

Katie looked at her in shock. Had she really said that? Share? Buddy? He was a nice guy, but that was all. What was this Julie even talking about?

Thankfully Dan appeared and led her to a seat. The teacher was about to start his lesson.

"What was Julie talking about?" Dan whispered as they sat down. "You looked a bit shocked."

"I was. It seems she and Buddy, from the book store, are an item. She doesn't share, and I'm to remember that." Katie rolled her eyes.

Dan laughed. "Sounds like Julie. She can get a little carried away."

"Dan," she whispered back. "You know Buddy is just a friend, don't you?"

"Of course I do." He reached for her hand. "Let's go to Rocky's after Sunday school and grab a bite for lunch. We'll talk more."

She squeezed his hand and smiled. Who cared what those stupid girls said. Dan was here beside her now, and hopefully for a long, long time in the future.

The class was okay, although Katie had a problem concentrating on the teacher's lesson on one of the parables. Julie and Angie sat together two rows ahead of them, and occasionally whispered back and forth, even looking back at her. Good grief, she thought. This wasn't fun at all. Dan, of course, appeared not to notice anything.

⁂ ⁂ ⁂

Later that afternoon Katie sat at the desk in her bedroom trying to study for a test in English class the next day. She had just re-read the three stories and was pondering what essay the teacher might have them write. They all seemed to have the idea of regret in them. So maybe that would be the topic she'd choose. She could certainly relate to it. She wished she had done better in her classes, and had graduated by now. She wished she and Dan had been married before she had gotten pregnant.

Then she looked down at her left hand and smiled. Sure there were regrets, but also now there was the future that suddenly looked so bright. She had been so surprised at lunch. The waiter had just swooped down on their table, clearing it quickly. Then Dan made a big show of digging into the pocket of his jacket.

"There's something here I can't forget," he had said with a chuckle. And then a little box was set on the table. "For you."

She looked at him in surprise. Was this a ring? It sure seemed to be. She had had no idea he'd choose today to spring this on her.

"Well," he prodded her. "Opening the box would be a first step!"

So she did. And what she saw made her so happy that tears came to her eyes. It was a small diamond on a silver band. Perfect. It actually reminded her of her grandmother's ring. She had always liked its elegant simplicity.

"Do you like it?"

"Like it? How about love it! You couldn't have picked out a more perfect ring."

Dan grinned. "I remembered what you once said about your grandma's ring, and how you liked the simplicity of it. So I looked all over, just for you."

"You couldn't have picked anything more perfect."

"So let's see if it fits." He lifted the ring from the box and put it on her finger. It fit. Of course. And more tears came. She didn't think she could be any happier than she was right now.

Then they talked about a wedding date, agreeing that in early September, before Bethel's classes started, would be perfect. This summer they'd look for an apartment in a new married housing development that was going to be available for the fall semester. Dan would check on that right away, and they would both sign up for classes soon. She had to pinch herself; was this really happening?

⁂ ⁂ ⁂

Now as Katie sat in her room looking at her ring, she heard a knock on the door.

"Hey Katie, Mom's fixing popcorn. Want any?"

Of course. Popcorn was their Sunday night ritual.

"Tom, come in." She hadn't had a chance to show Tom and their Mom the ring yet. "After we eat popcorn, could we talk, just you and me?"

"Sure. We'll chow down and then talk up here while Mom grades papers. Which she always does, you know."

So she went out to the living room, and they ate popcorn. Of course she showed off her ring and talked about her plans. Her mom and Tom seemed very happy for her.

After popcorn, she and Tom went to her room and sat around the desk there.

"I'm so happy for you and Dan," Tom said. "And I know Mom is, too."

Katie smiled. "But I've been thinking about what Angie said once."

"She said something good for a change?" Tom asked. "I mean, you and she don't exactly get along, right?"

"Right. But . . . she's right about what Dan needs. He needs someone who believes like he does."

"You mean about God. And Jesus."

She nodded.

"But Katie, how about you? What do you need? Is Dan forcing this on you?"

"Oh no. Far from it. He has been incredibly patient, and kind, and I love him for that."

She looked down at her hands, wondering what to say. And yes, what exactly did she want? "I guess this is what I want. I want what he has, what you and Mom have. You are all at peace about God. You seem to know Him. And me? I just don't have a clue what to do."

⁂ ⁂ ⁂

Later that night Katie sat on her bed and prayed. For the first time ever, she actually prayed because now she knew God was listening. One thing she prayed for was Tom. He had helped her to get a clue. Becoming a Christian was not checking off boxes of what she had to do. It was simply believing. Believing that Jesus died on the cross for our sins, that He rose from the dead and went to Heaven. That's all it took; just believing.

She remembered that Tom left the room once to get his Bible. He read John 3:16 to her: 'For God so loved the world that He gave His only begotten Son, that whoever believes in Him shall not perish but have eternal life." Romans 10:9-10: "If you confess with your mouth Jesus as Lord, and believe in your heart that God raised Him from the dead, you will be saved; for with the heart a person believes, resulting in righteousness, and with the mouth he confesses, resulting in salvation." Verse 13: 'Whoever will call on the name of the Lord will be saved."

"You know, the sermon this morning was really for me, I think," Katie said.

Tom smiled. "God seems to know when we need to really hear something. I mean, sometimes we hear but we don't really listen."

Katie nodded. "The pastor said a sentence that stood out to me: 'We don't believe because we don't want to believe.' I think that was me."

They sat for a moment longer, looking down at the Bible in Tom's hand. "You know," Katie said, "I'm lacking something."

"Really?" Tom asked.

"Yes. A Bible. Could you go shopping with me for one?"

"Let's talk to Mom," Tom suggested, "and all of us go shopping together. That will make her day."

Tears came to Katie's eyes, and they hugged before walking down the hallway to see her Mom.

CHAPTER SIXTEEN

FRANKLIN

The lot is cast into the lap, but its every decision is from the Lord.
Proverbs 16:33

But if any of you lacks wisdom, let him ask of God, who gives to all generously, and it will be given to him.
James 1:5

Franklin felt happy about life when he parked his car that early April morning. Spring had finally come to Michigan; he had only needed a light jacket that morning. And there were daffodils and crocuses lining the walkway into the school as he strolled in. A date for his marriage had been set. Life was good.

Then he checked his mailbox in the office. A note from Steve. Had he made up his mind yet about his new assistant golf coach? The superintendent was asking. Franklin sighed. Right. There was that.

Next stop: the cafeteria. He picked up his usual coffee, debated about adding a donut to the tray, gave in, and then moved on to the faculty office. He'd sit quietly and ask himself why he hadn't made a decision yet. He liked Nate; Nate golfed well and seemed to have a good rapport with his students. So what was the problem? Franklin sipped his coffee and took another bite of the chocolate donut. It was this whole Ralph thing, he decided. It was making him suspicious of everyone.

Pat sat her coffee down with a thump and startled him.

"Didn't mean to scare you," she said.

"Right. You love sneaking up on me to see what I'm doing wrong."

"Well, there is that donut again," she said with a knowing smile.

'Yeah. Some days we just need a little extra TLC."

"You mean you have problems?" Pat asked. "Can I tell you about mine?"

Then Emily sat down with her tea. "Problems? You two have problems? I could add some of mine to your list."

Franklin opened the note from Steve and showed it to the two women.

"Ah," said Emily. "Decision time. It's not Nate?"

"I kind of remember a couple of things you two related after Ralph died," Pat said. "Didn't Nate seem glad not to have Ralph around anymore causing problems?"

"True," Franklin said. "And then Emily over-heard him talking to another woman in the math office about not having to worry about payments any more. And we know Ralph had been black-mailing a few people; Nate and Sam seemed to be two of them."

"But nothing definite?" Pat asked.

"Right. Just enough to make me pause."

"So what will you do?" Emily asked.

"Well, I just heard yesterday about a guy – Jeff Barnes – in the Freshman wing. A good golfer, I was told." Franklin paused for another sip of coffee. "I'm debating things in my mind. Maybe I should just casually talk to Jeff and see what I think?"

"Good plan," Pat said, standing up and waving good-bye. "And good luck."

Emily stood up also. "Time to go. But Franklin, it sure can't hurt to talk to Jeff. It might give you the answer you're looking for. Oh, pray too."

Now why didn't I think of that, Franklin asked himself as he walked to his room. Sometimes talking to other people was really helpful.

After Franklin's last class of the day he decided to wander over to Emily's room. Kids were still milling around, slamming lockers shut and yelling at each other about plans for meeting later. Which was exactly why he wanted to see Emily.

He opened her door and found her writing notes in her planner. "Lots to do tonight?" Franklin asked. He noticed how her green sweater looked cheery, and good on her. But then everything looked good on her. She was very attractive, and Franklin thought again what a lucky guy he was.

"Oh, pretty much the usual," she replied.

"Maybe you need a break before tackling all those essays?"

"Of course," she said, smiling. "I'll pack things up and be ready in a jiffy."

"Shall we meet at the Starbucks for a change, the one on North?"

"Sure. Good idea. See you there."

❋ ❋ ❋

Ten minutes later they had ordered their drinks and were seated at a small table, in a row of tables, near the window. Franklin looked out at the parking lot, full of cars sitting in the sun. It was good to see the sun after so many cloudy winter days. It was good to see Emily. And he had some good news.

"I walked over to the Freshman wing on my prep hour," Franklin said. "Luckily I found Jeff in his classroom before his class started. He was writing some questions on the board about the planets; he's a science teacher you know. Anyway he agreed to meet tonight at Leon's pizza. When I said I wanted to talk about golf, his face lit up."

"A good sign," Emily said.

"I hope so. I'll sound him out, sort of beat around the bush. Not sure if I'll actually offer him the position. I'll see, I guess," Franklin said, drinking some of his black tea.

Emily smiled. "You'll know when it's time, I'm sure."

"On another subject. Pat showed me Ralph's obituary," Franklin said. "It mentioned Ralph's high school days playing football."

"Football can be so good for guys," Emily commented. "Too bad it didn't work for Ralph." She drank some tea and went on. "You know, when I talked to Steve recently I said I'd heard that his brother and Ralph had gone to school together. He was pretty quiet; didn't say much.

"And yet Ralph worked at the high school," Franklin said. "If Larry and Ralph had some big problems, I wonder why Steve would want him around the school. Seems awkward to me."

Emily nodded. "Could Ralph have pressured Steve to get the job at the high school? Maybe he even said he'd tell the press something about the old football days and bring doubt on the mayor's character. Steve wouldn't want his brother to go through all that."

Franklin thought about that. "I suppose that's as good a theory as any."

Emily nodded. "Well, it's probably time to get going."

They both stood up and walked out the door.

"I hope all goes well with Jeff," Emily said as she reached her car. See you tomorrow."

❋ ❋ ❋

An hour and a half later Franklin had driven home, changed his clothes, read the paper, and then headed to Leon's Pizza. He found a table against the wall, where numerous pictures of Italy were hanging over it. He sat down and ordered a Coke. A few minutes later Jeff arrived, apologizing for being late.

"Oh, you're fine," Franklin said. "Guess I tend to be a little early."

"So I think it's great news that you'll be coming to the Freshman wing in the fall," Jeff said after he too ordered a Coke.

"Thanks, Jeff. I'm looking forward to it." Franklin quickly scanned the short menu. "I guess I'll just order a small sausage pizza. You might want the larger size, since you're still young and growing." He chuckled. "Just figured you'd want more than I want."

Jeff laughed. "Growing is right. Which is why I need to play all the golf I can."

Franklin didn't think Jeff looked even remotely over-weight. He was a nice looking guy in his jeans and navy sweater. But Franklin definitely understood the need to stay active.

"So when did you start playing golf?" Franklin asked.

"Seems like all my life. My dad taught me; we used to go out every Saturday when I was growing up, probably from the age of nine or ten. And then I was on the golf team in high school."

"Great. And where was that?"

"Up in Muskegon. Then I went to Western Michigan University and played golf there also, while getting my science degree."

The pizzas arrived and they were quiet while they took their first bites.

"So is this your first job since college?"

Jeff nodded as he chewed. "First job, and I'm loving it. By the way, great pizza, and good choice of places, too."

"I'm glad you like it here in Springton. I've been here about twenty-five years, so it seems to agree with me too."

Jeff chuckled. "Will you miss teaching classes next year?"

"You know, I really will miss that, as I told Steve when he offered me the job. So he opened the door for me." Franklin pushed the pizza plate to the side, finding that even a small one was more than he wanted or needed.

"So what door was opened?" Jeff asked.

"He said it might be possible to teach a class now and then if the student counts get high. He did say, however, that it was only a 'maybe.' Then he said I'd end up being surprised at how busy my new job would keep me."

They were quiet for a couple of minutes as Franklin gulped down some Coke. Then he took the plunge. "So I was wondering if you'd be interested in helping me with the golf team next year," Franklin said. "Assistant coach. Small pay, but still some dollars. And it's not for the full year, since we do get some snow around here. But Fall for sure and maybe Spring, as we're doing now."

Jeff also pushed away his plate and smiled widely. "You know, I can't think of anything I'd rather do. Thank you so much."

Franklin felt relief. This seemed right. Then the two of them started talking about details of the job.

❋ ❋ ❋

The next morning Franklin saw Nate in the hallway on his way to get the mail. He had decided last night, after calling Steve about Jeff, that he could tell Nate his decision was made for Jeff, since they would both be working in the Freshman wing. It seemed fairly logical to him. But would Nate think so?

"Nate, I was hoping I'd run into you right away," Franklin said after they had greeted each other in the hallway. Both of them moved to the side as a group of students came barreling down the hall. "Since I'm going to be in the Freshman wing next year, I decided it made sense to see if Jeff could help me with golf."

Nate immediately frowned. "You did? Oh, I thought... I mean I assumed you'd be asking me."

Franklin felt his heart drop. He hated these kinds of conversations, hated disappointing someone. What could he say?

"Well, I think this will work out with both of us in the same building. I'm sorry it isn't the way you had hoped."

"Franklin!"

Franklin turned to see Steve walking rapidly down the hall.

"Could I see you in your room as soon as you're done here?" Steve asked. Then he turned and walked toward Franklin's room.

"Sorry, again," Franklin said. "I'd better see what crisis Steve has for me."

He quickly turned and trotted toward his room, relieved that he had an excuse to end the conversation. Nate looked upset. More than upset. Mad. Even livid. Oh brother, he thought.

Steve was standing in the doorway of his room talking to a couple of students. "I thought I might as well let them in," he told Franklin. Everything okay?"

"Well, I told Nate about Jeff. He's very upset."

"That's what I noticed when I was coming down the hall. Thought maybe you could use a break," Steve said.

"Good timing," Franklin admitted. "It's so awkward when you're turning someone down."

"So, gut feeling. Right decision?"

Franklin smiled. "Very right. Thanks again."

CHAPTER SEVENTEEN

EMILY

But as for me, I shall sing of Your strength; yes I shall joyfully sing of Your lovingkindness in the morning. For you have been my stronghold and a refuge in the day of my distress.

Psalm 59:16

My life is going to be changing so much this year. I'll marry Franklin in June. I think Katie will marry Dan in late August and then go to Bethel with him. Tom will be headed back to school in September. And now, through a journal from my late mother, I'll get to hear Mom's voice again. I have missed her so much; I can't wait to sit down and devour that journal.

It was a normal Wednesday morning in mid-April. Emily was standing at her classroom door greeting students as they came in. First hour was an English 10 honors class. Bright students, and very nice for the most part. There was always a snarky teenage girl or two, or a full-of-himself guy on the football team to contend with. She had come to expect all kinds.

"I love this book," Cynthia said as she walked in. "To Kill a Mockingbird is my favorite this year!"

"Oh, good," Emily said. "Atticus is a great person, don't you think?"

Cynthia nodded and hurried off to chat with her friends.

"Mrs. Sanderson," whined Ellie as she walked in, "is this the last boring book we have to read this semester? I don't know how I'll make it to the end!"

Emily just patted her on the shoulder. "You'll end up liking it, I bet."

Ellie kept frowning as she went to plop her books on her desk.

You just can't please everybody, Emily thought. Fortunately she hadn't come across too many like Ellie.

She went back out to the hallway, and just then she spotted Nate coming in from the parking lot. "Thanks again for helping us with the dance," she said as he came near.

He stopped by her door. "Of course."

"Isn't this a great spring day?" Emily asked.

"Not really," Nate replied. "I've been told I won't be a golf coach next year, and I'm really bummed. I'm off to talk to Steve about it."

With that, Nate hurried away, looking as if he were ready to really unload on Steve. It was times like this when she was glad she was a teacher and not an assistant principal, Emily thought as she closed the door and got ready to start a discussion on Atticus.

⁂ ⁂ ⁂

After morning classes Emily grabbed her purse, locked the door, and walked to the faculty lunchroom to retrieve her lunch from the fridge. She found a corner table and spread out her lunch, such as it was, to try to save seats for Franklin and Pat. She usually brought a yogurt and apple from home, unlike Franklin and Pat who got something yummy from the cafeteria. She figured if she could avoid looking at all the possible choices she'd save herself both calories and money.

Pat and Franklin came in with their trays piled with salad for Pat and a chicken pot pie for Franklin. Emily sighed, looked at her yogurt, and started spooning it in. It was okay, she told herself.

"We just saw Steve," Franklin said. "He asked us to save him a seat."

Emily raised her eyebrows. This wasn't normal. Steve usually had a hamburger on the run as he walked around checking things out and talking to students.

"I saw Nate this morning," Emily said as the others started eating. "Not a happy camper. 'Really bummed' were his actual words."

Franklin nodded. "I know. He wasn't pleased with me at all when I told him Jeff would be the assistant coach next year. I knew I had to tell him, but it sure wasn't easy."

Just then Steve showed up and sat down, hamburger in hand. He took a bite before he spoke. "Franklin, did you ever promise Nate the coaching job?"

"Absolutely not. Is that what he told you?" Franklin looked disgusted.

Steve nodded, chewing another bite. "But that's not all. Should I go on?" Steve looked around the table. "Or we can talk in private."

"Go ahead," Franklin said. "The room is almost empty, and these two know everything about me."

Steve lowered his voice. "Nate claims you're not managing the golf funds right. As in skimming off the top."

Franklin's mouth opened in surprise. "He said what?"

Emily said, "You've got to be kidding."

Pat was so shocked she couldn't seem to get any words out of her mouth.

"Steve, I'll be glad to show you the books. But there's not much to show. The board gives very little money for golf meets, and it's always gone by the end of the season."

"I totally trust you, Franklin," Steve said, throwing his hamburger paper in the waste basket nearby. "But bring the books in after school. Nate made a serious charge and I want to stop it in its tracks. I'll have someone from the main office there, also."

Steve stood up. "Don't worry. We'll get to the bottom of this." Then he left.

Emily looked at Pat, then at Franklin. "I just can't believe this. You're the most honest person I know."

"I totally agree," Pat said. "Please let us know if there's something we can do. Like go beat up Nate until he tells the truth."

"You're great friends." He smiled. "Maybe we can put off the beating until later, though."

Emily looked at her watch and stood up. "I'm glad you have only two more classes this afternoon. I'll wait after school in my room until you're done with Steve."

❋ ❋ ❋

After her last class, Emily did some planning for the next day and figured out what she should take home to grade. Her briefcase was always full of papers – one of the benefits of being an English teacher. Ha! She looked at the clock. Franklin had been in Steve's office no more than a half hour. Maybe he'd stop in soon.

Then she looked around her room. Much of her world was here with these desks, books, and posters. Right now she couldn't imagine a life without teaching; she loved it. As she circled the room with her eyes, one new poster stood out, and she smiled. She had put it up just for fun, wondering if anyone would notice and try to figure it out. It had two panels on it, one underneath the other, with identical pictures. Or were they identical? The idea was to find six differences in the two pictures. It wasn't as easy as it sounded. And only one person so far had actually solved the puzzle. Emily had asked her to keep it a secret for a while to see if others could find the differences.

Suddenly she heard voices coming down the hall, which had been quiet once all the students had fled for the buses. There was a knock at the door; then Betty from the business department peeked around the corner. She was with another business teacher – Maryanne.

"We just wanted you to know about the rumor," Betty said.

Emily smiled and pointed to the desks, inviting them to sit. "Come on in and have a talk." The three sat down at the student desks and Emily asked, "So are these good or bad rumors?"

"Not good. Listen, I can't stay but a minute," Betty said. "The baby sitter will be anxious for me to get home. But both Maryanne and I thought you should know. Nate is complaining about Franklin, saying some awful things."

"No doubt untruthful things," Maryanne added. "We know Franklin. He's such a good guy."

"Agree," said Betty. "We don't like what Nate is doing, and certainly don't believe him." She paused. "He's been such a strange duck lately. I wonder what happened to him."

"So he doesn't usually go around cutting people down?" Emily asked.

"Right. But in the last year . . . He's been different somehow," Betty said.

Emily stood up. "Thanks, ladies. I have an idea what's going on. It was nice of you to tell me this. And I have complete faith in Franklin; hopefully this will all get sorted out soon."

Betty and Maryanne gave Emily a brief hug and left the room.

Then Franklin came in. "Having a party in here?" he kidded.

"As usual," Emily smiled. "And how did it go?"

"Steve and one of the assistant superintendents looked everything over and found nothing out of place with the golf club funds." Franklin sat down at one of the desks. "I never thought a fellow teacher would be treating me this way."

"And that's not all." Then she told him about the girls' visit.

"Oh boy," Franklin said. "Now everyone will know there are problems somewhere."

"What can be done?" Emily wondered.

"Steve will tell Nate he found nothing wrong and ask that he not say anything more about it."

"Yeah, right." Emily said. "Like that will make a difference. I think he's out for revenge."

Franklin shrugged, looking a bit down and out.

"There is something we can do, though." She went over and closed the door. "Let's pray a minute, and ask God to give us strength through this trial."

⁂ ⁂ ⁂

Later that night, after dinner with Katie and Tom, and after grading a stack of papers, Emily turned to her mom's journal that had finally arrived yesterday. There hadn't been time to give it a good read yet. She went to her room and sat in the rocker by the window, turned on the light, and started the journey into the past.

CHAPTER EIGHTEEN

TOM

By this all men will know that you are My disciples, if you have love for one another. John 13:35

Bear one another's burdens, and thereby fulfill the law of Christ. Galatians 6:2

As Tom parked and walked into the hospital that April morning, he started thinking about golf. He was surprising himself. He had only dabbled in golf occasionally before Franklin came into the picture. Which was odd, considering he had worked for a golf company, he chuckled to himself. But he had never had time before. Or maybe never made the time? Ever since Franklin had asked him and Nate to go out to the course, he had found himself wondering if perhaps he could improve his game with more practice, plus Franklin's help.

These April days were enticing – sunny and temperatures in the 70s. Beautiful weather. Why waste it?

So he stopped outside the double doors, took out his phone, and called Franklin. Luckily Franklin had just gotten to school and was unlocking his door. He sounded really happy to hear from Tom, and yes he'd love to do a round of golf as soon as Tom left the hospital that day.

With a sigh of satisfaction, Tom rode the elevator to the third floor and as usual checked in with Nurse Cheryl. "I bet there are no problems today, right?" he asked Cheryl, chuckling a little. Of course there were problems. After all it was a hospital.

"Really?" Cheryl asked. "You've got to be kidding. Right now there is an elderly man in room 303. He's obnoxious and mean and demanding, and we're at our wit's end."

"Shall I start there?"

"Please! Right now he won't take his meds. Says the nurses are poisoning him. He's having a procedure done this morning, but needs to take those meds soon."

He hurried off, after taking the pill bottle from Cheryl, wondering if there was anything he'd be able to do to get the pill in the man. As he walked down the hall he sent up a quick prayer to God, asking for wisdom.

Tom stopped outside of Room 303, straightened his shoulders as if getting ready for battle, and sauntered in, not wanting to surprise him. He noticed on the wall opposite the bed a sign with the man's name – Edwin Rogers. Mr. Rogers had the TV on and was watching an old episode of MASH.

"Hello, Mr. Rogers," Tom said, peering around the corner. "I've come to see if there is anything I can do to help. Or is there anything I could get you? Coffee, cookies?"

Mr. Rogers frowned, but didn't say anything at first. His eyes stayed focused on the TV, where Hawkeye and BJ were eating and making fun of the army breakfast.

"So do you think the breakfasts here are any better than what Hawkeye had to eat?" Tom asked, hoping to get him to talk.

"Humph," the old man said. "It's lousy here. Everything is lousy. Even the coffee. Might as well be back in the army."

"So you were in the army too?"

"Yeah. I know what those army breakfasts are like."

"So what was the worst thing about them?" Tom asked.

"Everything was bland and stale and overcooked. Hardly worth eating."

"You know," Tom said. "I've heard the coffee down in the cafeteria is better than it is up here. Good chocolate chip cookies too I hear. Shall I get some for you?"

"You'd do that?"

"Well, sure. I'll be right back, maybe before Colonel Potter comes in to eat."

"So you like MASH too?"

"Love it. Used to watch it with my dad." Then Tom waved and hurried out of the room.

Five minutes later he was back. He put coffee and one cookie on the tray, wrapping the other two in a baggie, and looked up at the TV. This time Radar was helping Hawkeye call his dad back in the states.

Mr. Rogers took a sip of coffee and actually gave Tom a little smile. "Not bad, young man. That was mighty nice of you."

Tom smiled back. "And I've got a little pill for you to take with that cookie."

"It's not from that old biddy nurse, is it? Because I'm sure she's trying to poison me."

"Oh no," Tom said with his fingers crossed behind his back. "The doctor told me this would help your headache."

"Yeah, the headache is awful." Then Mr. Rogers swallowed the pill and bit into the cookie. "You're right. These are good."

"Great! These other cookies are for you to have later."

A commercial came on and Tom decided to see if Mr. Rogers wanted to talk a little more. "So have you watched MASH for a long time?"

"Oh yes, since the 70s I think. The kids and I used to tune in every Thursday night."

"So you have some kids. How old are they?"

"Yep. Two boys. Both in their forties by now. One in California and one in North Carolina."

"That's far from Michigan," Tom noted. "I suppose you don't see them too often?"

"No, but I'm having an operation. Today I think. The one in California – Scott – may be coming in later today."

"That's good news," Tom said. "So can I get anything else for you before I leave? I think Nurse Cheryl has more work for me."

"I'm sure she does." He laughed. "No, I'm fine. Thanks for the good coffee."

Tom smiled and left the room, wondering what Cheryl would have for him next. At the nurse's station, Cheryl was talking to someone new. "He took the pill," Tom said. "Piece of cake!" He grinned.

"Tom, meet Lori, our new nurse on this floor."

They exchanged smiles. She was young, probably just out of nursing school. Easy to look at. Soft brown hair pulled back in a small bun.

Cheryl went on. "Tom is our magic man. He has a way with tough patients, and we depend on him."

Tom laughed. "It's this spell I put on them. Works every time."

"Or, it's something you put in the cookies?" Cheryl asked.

"Could be." Tom smiled mysteriously. "So what can I do now?"

The rest of the day went like that. He took patients to surgery, including Mr. Rogers, and talked to others who seemed worried and upset. He also had a chance to talk to Lori. The two of them were in the break room at the same time in the middle of the afternoon. She mentioned liking it here in Springton, saying she was surprised at finding a couple of good golf courses around town, almost as good as those in Grand Rapids. His ears perked up at that. She liked golf? That could be interesting. But then Cheryl texted him with another job. So he had no chance to pursue the golf idea. Maybe later.

Before he knew it the day was over and it was time to head to Franklin's apartment.

⁂ ⁂ ⁂

By the time Tom returned home after golfing, it was after 7:00. He was ravenous. He stowed his clubs in the garage, then stood in front of the fridge to see if he could scrounge up something to eat.

"Hey, Tom," Emily called from her room where she was grading papers. "There is some chicken stew in the crock pot on the counter."

"Thanks, Mom. I see it now."

He got a bowl from the cupboard, scooped it full of stew, found a spoon in the drawer, and sat down at the kitchen table. "This is great, Mom," he called to her.

Emily appeared in the doorway a few minutes later. "So how was your golf game?" she said, sitting down.

Tom swallowed some stew. "I didn't do too badly I guess. But most important, it was fun. Franklin is a good teacher. We did lots of talking, too. He's a good guy, Mom."

Emily smiled. "He sure is. And anything exciting happen at work today?"

"Well, I don't know about exciting. The usual patients who need extra care." Then he told her about Mr. Rogers.

"He sounds like a nice guy, though," Emily said. "Maybe lonely. I hope his son from California was able to get here."

"Yes, he was actually nice once I got talking. That MASH show helped. But sometimes the nurses don't have time for TLC, so that's what my job is."

"Sounds like you'll be missed next fall when you go back to school," Emily observed.

"I'll see how the classes go. Maybe I'll be able to work part time. I'd like that. And what's new with you?"

"Big news. I've started reading my mom's journal."

"Yes?" Tom prodded.

"I may have a half-sister in San Diego."

"What? That's huge. So tell me more." Tom went back to the crock pot for seconds and then filled a glass with water.

"It is huge. When I read it, I had a hard time believing it," Emily said. "You know, a person has certain ideas about what life was like for her Mom and Dad. Mom always seemed to be the type to do everything just-so, and right. Obviously I knew nothing about my 'real' mom."

"I suppose that's true with most people," Tom said. "I would imagine I have no idea what your life was like when you were younger."

"True. There are lots of things we don't want to talk about with our children, I guess." Emily stopped and seemed to think about that. "So my mom got pregnant when she was a senior in high school. And in those days that wasn't acceptable at all. The girls were usually sent away to live for a few months. High school girls didn't keep going to school when they got pregnant, as they seem to do now."

"I remember a couple of girls in my graduating class who were pregnant at graduation," Tom said, thinking back. "People seemed to look at it as almost normal. I wonder now what happened to them."

"So my mom had a baby girl. She saw the baby once before she was adopted."

"That must have been so hard," Tom said.

Emily nodded. "I know. It's something that is hard for me to imagine. Having a baby and then never seeing her again? My mom must have been heart-broken. I wonder if it was something she thought about every day of her life after that."

"I suppose it's a bit like what Katie must be going through, since her baby died."

Emily nodded. "Anyway, last year my mom and dad decided to try to find her. I never heard about any of this. Maybe she decided she'd tell me if she found out anything. But the important thing is that they actually found her."

"No kidding. It must be easier to track those things down than in the old days. Didn't there used to be confidentiality laws?"

"True. Apparently things have changed. The little girl was called Angel. She's four years older than I am, and she lives in San Diego."

"So did your mom and dad ever see or talk to her?"

"Not really. The adoption agency had contacted Angel, and Angel had agreed to a visit. That's as far as it got, because they had that car accident last year, right before they were going to fly to San Diego."

"So close," Tom said.

They were quiet for a few moments. Tom got up to clean his bowl and set it in the dishwasher.

"I've been thinking of looking her up," Emily finally said.

"Really? That would be interesting, I guess. But hard too?" Tom asked. "Like what if she turns out to be hard to talk to? Maybe she doesn't want to think about how she was adopted. She might even hate her birth mother."

"I guess there are many ways this possible meeting could go," Emily said. "I'll have to think about it. Talk it over with Franklin."

"So her name is Angel. Last name?"

"Tompkins."

"Hmm. Tompkins. Someone at school has that last name, right?"

Emily thought a moment. "You have a good memory. Yes, it's Nate in the Business Department, the one you went golfing with. But it's probably a common name, don't you think?"

"No doubt," Tom said. But wouldn't that be funny if Nate were somehow connected to Angel, he thought. But then he brushed that thought away as being too ridiculous.

CHAPTER NINETEEN

KATIE

I will give You thanks with all my heart; I will sing praises to You before the gods . . . and give thanks to Your name for Your lovingkindness and Your truth. Psalm 138: 1-2

As Katie drove her old beat-up car to the bookstore on a gray April morning, she noticed something coming down on the windshield. Snow. Seriously, she thought? What was the matter with this Michigan weather?

But by the time she drove into the parking lot and parked, it had turned to rain. She grabbed her purse and the package from the seat beside her and scurried to the building.

"Hey, Buddy," she called as she walked in. He was usually here by the time she arrived, manning the cash register for early customers.

"Hi Katie," Buddy replied. "I see you made it through the snow!"

"Can you believe it – in April?"

"Remember we live in Michigan," Buddy said with a laugh. "Dan said he has some history textbooks that need shelving."

"Okay." Katie went to the back room to hang up her jacket and stow her purse, then see if she could interrupt Dan in his office for a few minutes.

Dan looked up from the papers on his desk as Katie lightly knocked and opened the door. "Do you have a minute?"

He smiled. "For you, many minutes."

"I want to show you something that I bought last night," she said. "Mom and Tom helped me."

"Of course. What is it?"

She opened the bag and brought out a Bible.

He looked surprised. She didn't blame him. Who would have guessed a week ago that she'd be going to the store to purchase a Bible?

He picked it up and looked it over. "A study Bible. This is a good edition. Tom and your mom did a good job with this."

"Tom did more than help me get this Bible. I did lots of thinking about that sermon last Sunday," she said. "We talked about it that night. I told him how different I felt at your church, like I didn't belong. He told me how to belong; he showed me how to be like you, a Christian." Katie felt tears come to her eyes. She felt so grateful not only for Tom, but for Dan's patience with her as she had worked through this.

Dan reached out and gave her a big hug. There were tears in his eyes also. "I knew it would happen," he said.

❋ ❋ ❋

A couple of hours later, she and Buddy traded places for a change of pace. Actually it was a box of English/Spanish dictionaries that was the problem. The books weighed tons, and Buddy had noticed how hard it was for her to reach the top shelf with them.

So she was at the cash register when Angie walked in. She waved slightly at Katie, but didn't say anything. That was fine with her, Katie thought. No matter how often she went to church, Katie didn't think she'd ever measure up to Angie's standards of life, whatever they were.

As she rang up a student's purchase of 3x5 cards and pens, she noticed Angie was making her way toward Dan's office. That was interesting. Did Angie still think she could someday win him away from her? Did she not understand they were engaged? Oh stop it, she scolded herself. Dan had a right to talk to anybody he wanted without her getting paranoid.

She gave the student his change and lost track of Angie. It didn't matter. Then two more students came with things to buy and she forgot about her, until the third person in front of her was actually Angie herself.

"Oh, hi," Katie said, looking for the item that Angie wanted to buy. "Can I help you?"

"Yes, I have a message for Dan, if you wouldn't mind telling him. Ask him to call me, please. It's important." Then Angie looked around as if wondering who could hear her next comment. "And you need to give up on your relationship with Dan. Or else. He's definitely not the one for you. Or are you too dumb to see that?"

Katie stood there open-mouthed, in shock. What could she say? What should she say? She could think of some pretty bad retorts, but wait. Tom had helped her turn her life around, only last night. She couldn't let Angie get to her and then become as bad as she was.

"I'll tell Dan to call," Katie said quietly. Then she quickly left the cash register to find Buddy. Handling some heavy books sounded good to her right now.

Before she reached Buddy, Dan called to her. She hadn't noticed him over by the greeting cards. Apparently Angie hadn't either.

"Angie wants you to call her," she said.

"Yes I know. I heard."

Katie looked up at Dan, hearing the disgust in his voice. What else had he heard?

"I didn't mean to, but I heard everything," Dan said. "Has this happened before?"

She nodded, figuring he meant had Angie talked to her about her relationship with Dan.

"So Angie often comes across that harshly?"

"Yes, Dan, but don't worry. I can handle it." Katie knew they had been friends for a long time. It honestly bothered her that she could play a part in breaking up a friendship.

"Hey, Buddy, could you do the cash register for a while? Katie will be back in a minute."

Buddy nodded. Dan led Katie back to his office where he closed the door and took her in his arms.

"In four months we're getting married and moving to Mishawaka. We'll be starting a whole new life," Dan said, looking at her intently. "I want you to know how much I'm looking forward to that. Just you and me. Because you're the one for me, and I love you so much."

He gave her a small kiss and a big hug.

"I love you so much," she whispered. Then she left the room so she could relieve Buddy, and thanked God for bringing Dan to her.

⁂ ⁂ ⁂

Later, over a dinner of tacos and beans, Katie came up to speed with her family. She and Dan had spent several evenings making plans for the future, and she had missed out on some family dinners.

"Franklin is coming over after a while, and I want to get his take on a possible meeting with Angel," her mom said.

Katie looked up from her plate, ready to take another bite. "So who's Angel?"

"Oh, yeah," her mom said. "I forgot you weren't here when I told Tom about my mom's journal." Then Emily told her about her mother's pregnancy while in high school, the adoption, and then finding out that the baby, now four years older than Emily, was living in San Diego. And that Emily's parents had planned to go to San Diego before their accident last year put a stop to any meeting.

Katie was stunned, but she detected in her mother's face that this was welcome news. "So I guess I have an aunt," Katie said. "What an interesting story. And Mom, after what happened to me, I can hardly comprehend having to give up a baby for adoption. Grandma must have gone through so much."

Emily nodded. "You're right, of course. And to think I never knew any of this. It does put another perspective on life when I think back. That's something I've been pondering lately. I've pretty much decided on going to San Diego and talking to Angel myself. In memory of my parents, I guess."

"Oh, Mom, of course you should go. I bet Angel would like to know about how her birth mom felt after all these years."

"Katie that's a good point," Emily said. "So I'm doing it not only for my parents, but for Angel herself. And selfishly for me, too. I used to wonder what it would be like to have a brother or sister. I used to be jealous of my friends who had a sibling."

"There is one other possible problem," Tom said. "Just so you're prepared. What if she doesn't want to know anything about her past?"

"Good point, Tom," Katie said. "Have you considered that, Mom? I've read stories about adoption meetings, and not all of them are smooth and happy."

'You're both right," Emily said. "Except last winter she did agree that my parents could visit her. But I still need to be ready for whatever Angel wants."

"So would you go alone?" Katie asked.

Emily paused, and Tom spoke up. "I could take a few days off from the hospital," Tom said. "I'd be glad to make the trip with you."

Katie looked at Tom, surprised. She noticed that her mom looked relieved. "Tom, that's so nice of you. What do you think, Mom?"

"I would love it. I think I'll call the adoption agency tomorrow. My parents left all that information. I can see what their reaction would be, and what they would recommend."

Just then the doorbell rang, and Franklin came in. "Hi everyone! All my favorite people, right here," he exclaimed.

Katie looked at him, thinking how much she loved him. She was so happy that he was the one her mom wanted to marry.

CHAPTER TWENTY

FRANKLIN

For the enemy has persecuted my soul; he has crushed my life to the ground . . . Psalm 143:3

In You our fathers trusted; they trusted and You delivered them. To You they cried out and were delivered; in You they trusted and were not disappointed. Psalm 2:4-5

Franklin sat at his desk in his room after the last student from American history left. The quiet felt good after a hectic day. Each class had had good discussions, which Franklin appreciated, but everyone had been quite energetic and lively today. Spring was definitely in the air. Kids were getting a bit antsy. These next weeks until the end of school would be challenging, as usual. But now it felt good to sit at his desk in peace and quiet.

He glanced around the room and noticed a couple of dictionaries that someone had left out. Crossing the room to stow them in the bookcase, he had to pass THE closet. The closet where Ralph had been found. He hardly used it anymore; opening the door was such a vivid reminder of that scene. He decided that was another plus for his move to the Freshman wing. He could leave this room and all of its reminders of Ralph.

There was a small knock at the door, and Jose peered in. "Irene in the office asked me to bring this box down to you," Jose said.

"Oh sure. Thanks, Jose." Franklin took the box. "This might be the new golf shirts for next year. Say, Jose, come on in for a minute. I was thinking of you and your wife recently, about citizenship."

Jose looked at him, puzzled. "Remember, it's my wife, not me," he said. "She never wanted to pursue it for herself. Except now that her parents have both died, she has fewer reasons to want to go back and forth to Mexico now."

"Didn't you say once that a school attorney helped you with your papers years ago?"

"He sure did. A real nice guy."

"Would you mind if I asked the attorney we have today if he could do the same for your wife?"

Jose smiled. "Maybe that's a good idea. She might agree to it now."

"Okay. I'll see what I can do. And thanks for the box," Franklin said.

As Jose left, Franklin went to his desk drawer to get the knife he kept there. These boxes were always so tightly taped up that he usually needed something sharp to get them open. Hm…

No knife. Odd. He never put it anywhere else except in the back of this drawer. Oh well, he'd use the scissors.

Then, as he was lifting the shirts out of the box, it occurred to him. Ralph was killed with a knife. In this room. Could it have been his knife? He thought back to finding Ralph. No, he had only seen Ralph propped up against the wall. He never saw the knife wound. He remembered the police saying the weapon seemed to be a small knife.

Just then there was another knock on the door. This time it was Steve.

"Hi Franklin," Steve said as he entered the room. "New golf shirts, I see; they look sharp."

"Yep. Just came today."

"Louie, from the police department, is in the office. Has a question for you. I'll walk you down."

Franklin locked the door and they started down the hall. "I just talked to Jose. He thinks his wife would be agreeable to look into her possible citizenship. Do you suppose our school attorney could help, like Jose was helped years ago?"

"Very likely," Steve said. "I'll be glad to look into it." He was silent for a moment. "But right now we have a more pressing problem. It has to do with a knife."

Franklin looked at him in surprise. "What a coincidence. I was just looking for an old kitchen knife I always had in the back of my top drawer in the desk."

"It's not there?"

"No, which is odd. I always put it right back when I use it," Franklin said.

"And Ralph was found with a knife wound in his neck, in your room," Steve said.

"Doesn't sound good, does it? That's a problem, all right."

"So Louie said that the police received an anonymous phone call. The person said you kept a knife in your desk drawer, and shouldn't he be a suspect? Meaning you."

"Oh boy. That doesn't look good. So now the police think I ……"

"No, no," Steve interrupted. "They're just following up on the tip."

By this time they were outside of Steve's office.

"Steve, you don't think I had anything to do with it, do you?"

"Absolutely not." Steve patted him on the back and they went in to face Louie.

An hour later, after the short talk with Louie, Franklin was at Emily's helping her eat some leftover spaghetti.

"Thanks for dinner, Emily. After my day at school I needed some good old-fashioned spaghetti," Franklin said. During dinner Franklin had told her all about the knife and Louie's talk with him.

"You're welcome, but it was only leftovers," Emily said, getting up to put their plates in the sink. "Tom and Katie are both out, so I hadn't planned anything."

"Leftovers are good. Sometimes better the second time around."

"You know, I have a thought about the knife," Emily said. "I bet it was the killer who called the police. Who else would know you kept a knife in your desk, except the very person who was frantically looking for a weapon."

"Hm… I guess it does make sense."

"Sure. It puts the blame on you," Emily said.

Just then the doorbell rang, and Emily went to the door, then brought Steve into the kitchen. "Just in time for brownies," she said.

"Sounds great," Steve said, sitting down opposite Franklin. "Just thought I'd see how you're doing. Took a lucky guess and found you here."

"It's hard to fool you, I guess," Franklin chuckled. "Emily and I were hashing over the day."

"Louie believes you, you know," Steve said as he reached for a brownie. "I mean he didn't exactly say that; but I could tell. He just has to do his job and follow up on all the clues."

"Thanks, Steve, and I do understand what he's doing."

"So now we need to figure out who was in the room with Ralph," Emily said. She put more brownies on the plate and sat down herself. "You know, I wonder why he was ever hired in the first place."

"Well," Steve said after a pause. "I can help with that one. And this goes back to when Ralph was in high school." He took a bite and thought a minute.

"Right here in Springton, right?" Franklin asked.

"Yes. My brother and I also went to this high school. I was a couple of years ahead of them."

"And your brother and Ralph were on the football team," Emily said.

"Right. That's where so much of this begins." Steve took some Coke from Emily and smiled his thanks. "One year a player died in summer practice because of something that was put in his water. Ralph and this football player had been vying for the same position on the team, so some people blamed Ralph, saying he wanted to stop the competition. Then Ralph turned around and blamed Larry, my brother, saying that Larry had also wanted that certain position."

"Wow," said Emily. "Sounds like quite a mess. So what happened?"

"The death was finally ruled accidental. There was just no proof. Most people actually thought Ralph might have been behind it; he had a bad reputation even then. But still, no proof."

"So your brother finally became mayor," Franklin said. "Is that when Ralph re-entered the picture?"

"Actually, yes," Steve said. "He came to me one day, claiming to have problems getting a job. Said if I hired him he wouldn't make problems for Larry, who was running for re-election that year." Steve put his hands on the table. "He sort of had me there. I didn't want to see Larry lose an election because of that guy and some rumors from years ago in high school. So, yes, I hired him, and hated what I saw him doing to people. He was so sneaky. Always looking where someone might be vulnerable and then getting him to pay up to stop rumors."

"Sounds like you were between a rock and a hard place where Ralph was concerned," Franklin said.

"No kidding. I was able to keep him in other schools in the district, so I wouldn't have to see him," Steve said. "But obviously that was hard to do all the time."

"Look, it's getting late," Steve said, looking at his watch. I'd better move along."

They all stood up, and Emily and Franklin walked Steve to the door.

"We'll get this all figured out," Steve said. "Don't worry."

After they closed the door and walked back into the kitchen, Emily asked him if he was still worried.

Franklin nodded. "I'll probably not rest easy until we figure out who the real killer is."

"God knows," Emily said. She took his hands in hers. "Let's pray together, and ask Him for help. We need to remember that He has all the answers."

CHAPTER TWENTY ONE

EMILY

Though I walk in the midst of trouble, You will revive me; You will stretch forth Your hand against the wrath of my enemies, and Your right hand will save me. The Lord will accomplish what concerns me; Your lovingkindness, O Lord, is everlasting; do not forsake the works of Your hands.

Psalm 138: 7-8

When I look at my life right now I try to concentrate on the positives. It would be easy to get too worked up over finding Ralph's murderer. Especially because now we think he was killed with Franklin's knife. I have no doubts about Franklin, but I'm scared for him. This can't be easy for him to know that people wonder if he was the one. On the positive side I'm looking forward to continuing Mom's search for her adopted baby. I like thinking that I can help my mom, even though she's not with us anymore.

Emily sat in the faculty lounge with her yogurt and apple, alone at the table next to the window, waiting for Pat and Franklin to come from the lunch line. She liked this table where she could look out over the school courtyard at the garden cared for by the students in a Home Ec. class. Tulips were almost ready to pop; by May they would surround the small square filled with herbs and vegetables.

"Hi Emily," Pat said as she and Franklin joined her at the table, carrying their lunch trays. "More problems, I'm afraid."

"More?" Emily asked. "Wait a minute; I don't want any more."

"Sorry. I checked our sophomore class account book in the office," Pat said.

"Something wrong? Did Nate goof up?"

"It looks odd," Pat said with a frown, sipping her iced tea. "All the bills were paid after our Barefoot dance, so that's good"

"Okay, but what could be wrong with that?" Emily asked.

"There's no money left in our account. The dance was a success; it was well-attended. There should have been some leftover dollars that we could use next year."

"Oh brother," Emily said. "I'm so glad we asked a so-called money man to help us."

"I don't know what to do," Pat said.

"Steve should know," Franklin said. "And next time don't ask Nate. Even I could help," he added with a smile.

"Is this another way of getting back at you? I mean, we're connected; we're getting married in June, and he's mad at you." Emily wondered. "So maybe he's trying to do anything he can to get back at you."

"This is all my fault," Pat said. "It all started at a faculty meeting. I remember talking in a small group of teachers about the pains of keeping the sophomore class books. I sure wish I'd kept my thoughts to myself."

"So Nate was there and kindly offered to help, I suppose," Franklin said.

"That's about it."

"But Pat," Emily said. "This isn't all your fault. I agreed, and thought it was a good idea. Now, of course, we know better."

Just then Nate walked by the table. "Hey Nate," Emily called to him.

"Hello, Emily," he said, looking puzzled.

"Could Pat and I come to your office after school? We have a question about the sophomore class account."

Nate seemed to consider a moment. "Sorry. I'm busy today, and besides there's nothing to talk about. Bills were all paid, and the account is now zero." Then he turned and walked out of the lounge.

All three of them looked at each other in disbelief.

"I can't believe what just happened," Emily said, shaking her head.

"Very strange," Franklin agreed. "He accuses me of tampering with the golf books and then he actually does the same thing with the sophomore class."

"I'm going to see Steve after school," Pat said. "Something is not right. Maybe we're not talking about a lot of money here, but still . . ."

"Shall I come with you?" Emily asked.

"Sure. See you later, and I'd better get to class now."

With that, they all departed.

⁂ ⁂ ⁂

Later, after school, Emily stopped at the grocery to get something for dinner, deciding on chicken and rice for a casserole. Then she hurried home to put it together for Tom and Katie. It wouldn't be long, she thought as she took grocery bags into the kitchen, before there would be four of us every night. The thought made her smile. And then she remembered. Katie and Tom would be moving in the fall. So there would be just two for dinner. Still, something to smile about.

Once dinner was in the oven, Katie and Tom came strolling in the door. They opened the refrigerator for drinks, and then sat down at the table to talk. She told them the latest about Nate, and about the talk with Steve.

"Steve seemed a bit down about our news about the sophomore class funds," Emily said. "He's had so many negative things happen lately, and this is almost like the last straw, I guess."

"With the murder of Ralph on his mind, he must be keeping very busy," Tom observed.

"You're right. And no real progress yet." Emily stood up to take the casserole out of the oven.

Katie started putting a small salad together. "So how did your talk end?" she asked.

"Interesting. Both Pat and I told him this wasn't that big a deal. We said we could just let it go for now, considering all he had on his plate with the murder." Somehow that had seemed like the thing to do.

Emily put plates on the table while Tom got the silverware out. "He seemed a bit relieved, but glad we had let him know."

"But what if you need start-up money next fall?" Tom asked.

"Good question. He assured us he'd help us out if we needed it."

"Maybe Nate won't be back next year?" Tom asked.

Emily looked at him, thinking. "Wouldn't that be nice? He sure doesn't seem happy now at Springton High. Oh, well." Emily decided that was just wishful thinking. There were other things to worry about.

They sat down to eat, and Emily prayed before they ate.

"So what about the adoption agency?" Katie asked.

Emily swallowed some chicken. Really good, she thought. "I called as soon as I got home from school, and the director said she would talk to Angel right away."

"When would you want to go?" Tom asked.

"Well, what if we could meet her this weekend? Would that be possible for you? Maybe we could fly over Saturday and come back Sunday?"

"Sure. Works for me. I'll check with the hospital of course."

Emily smiled. She'd see what Angel's response was. Her mom would have been pleased.

CHAPTER TWENTY TWO

TOM

The Lord sustains all who fall and raise up all who are bowed down. The eyes of all look to You, and You give them their food in due time. You open Your hand and satisfy the desire of every living thing. Psalm 145:14-16

Tom and Emily sat in the restaurant in the Holiday Inn, relaxing after the plane ride from Chicago to San Diego.

"So far, so good," Emily said. "No problem with the flight, and we have adjoining rooms that look comfortable. I was able to contact the adoption agency, and they talked to Angel; I called Angel and confirmed with her that we could meet here. Everything is good."

"You sound like you expected problems," Tom laughed. "Remember, your mom and you thought this out thoroughly. And we all prayed. God is watching over us."

Emily laid her hand on his arm. "Good point. I need to think positive." She took a sip of the water on the table. "And I thank you again for coming with me. It really makes me feel more comfortable."

"Someone is headed to our table. It looks like your sister. No really, she looks like you!" Tom exclaimed.

Emily glanced at Tom. "Really?"

"Really. Almost hard to believe."

And then Angel was there beside them. Emily stood. The two women started to shake hands; then Emily gave her a big hug.

"Please sit down. I'm Emily, of course, and this is my son, Tom. He was right a minute ago. We really do look like sisters."

Angel laughed and sat down. "Thank you for coming all the way out here to see me. That was so nice of you."

"Once I read mom's journal, after she died, I knew I had to look you up. She was so excited that she had found you."

"If only the timing could have been different. It would have been wonderful to meet your parents. I've always wondered about my mom, what she was like, and what the circumstances were that I was adopted by another family. But I guess that's the way it is," Angel said.

"I've got some pictures to show you," Emily said. "Pictures of our mom. Oh Angel, she wanted so much to see you."

The two women then talked and talked. One would never have thought that they had just met. It made him feel so good to see the happiness on his mom's face. And they did look so much like sisters. They were about the same height, with short light brown hair. They both wore slacks and a nice top, and both outfits were shades of blue.

They managed to order salads, both of them, while Tom ordered a steak sandwich. His meal was excellent, but while he was happily shoving the last bite in his mouth, he noticed that the women had barely made a dent in their salads. The meeting seemed to be very successful. How interesting, he thought, that two people who had never met before could have so much to discuss.

And then the subject of jobs came up. Angel was a hair stylist, which led to a discussion of hair styles on women over fifty. No controversy there. Then Emily started talking about being an English teacher at Springton High. Surely a safe subject. But Angel's face showed otherwise. Emily seemed oblivious, and she started talking about To Kill a Mockingbird, and the Barefoot dance, and her fiancé who was a history teacher.

Then Angel abruptly asked a question. "Is there more than one high school in Springton,"

"Why no, only one," Emily said.

"Is there a Nate who works there?"

Tom's ears perked up. Angel and Nate had the same last name. A connection?

"Yes," Emily answered. "Nate Tompkins." She paused a moment. "You both have the same last name. Do you know him?"

Angel paused. "Do I ever. He's a cousin of mine. My adopted dad's brother's son."

Tom didn't think she looked very happy about admitting this relationship.

"Ah," Emily said. "Yes, he works in the business department."

"So what do you think of him?"

Emily glanced at Tom. Probably wondering what she could say that wouldn't hurt Angel's feelings.

"Well, I guess we haven't exactly seen eye-to-eye on everything," Emily said.

Tom understood that his mom felt boxed in. She really didn't like Nate at all. After all, he lied about Franklin's handling of the golf accounts; he had, maybe, done something wrong with the sophomore class accounts; plus he had been black-mailed by Ralph after a seemingly inappropriate relationship with a physical education teacher. It didn't leave much to like about the guy.

"Don't feel bad about saying that, Emily," Angel said. "He's not a favorite person in our family."

"Oh, well, I'm certainly sorry to hear that," Emily said. "I guess there's always some family member who doesn't quite measure up in our eyes."

"Well, the problem is that he didn't treat my son right," Angel said.

"Oh you have a son also!" Emily said. "I guess we hadn't gotten that far in our talk."

"Yes. Gary is a senior in college, majoring in environmental science, and golfing every chance he can."

Tom's ears perked up again. A golfer in his mom's newly-found family. That was interesting.

Emily looked at Tom. "We both have golfing sons. Actually Tom is just getting into it, but he seems to really like it. Interesting, isn't it? Two sisters who have sons who golf. But back to Nate. I'm sorry Nate didn't treat Gary very well. That's hard when a family member does that."

"It sure is," Angel said. "Gary worked for Nate one summer in his landscaping business, and he wasn't paid for all the hours he worked."

"Ouch," Emily said. "And with Gary in college, I'm sure he needed all he could get."

"Absolutely," Angel said. "Hair stylists aren't exactly getting the highest salaries in the country, so I needed Gary to help pay for college."

Emily nodded in understanding. There was a pause in the conversation.

"You know, Angel, this has been so wonderful meeting you. I'm so sorry our mom couldn't have been here."

"Oh, for me, too," Angel said. "I've loved knowing more about my mom, and about the sister I never knew I had."

"We don't leave until tomorrow afternoon," Emily said. "Do you suppose the two of us could have brunch in the morning? I know Tom was thinking of trying out the golf course next door. Would Gary perhaps like to do that also?"

"Great," Angel said. "I'll have to check with Gary, but I'm betting he'll jump at the chance to meet you two and also golf."

Tom smiled. "That sounds perfect; I'd love to meet him."

❋ ❋ ❋

On the way back to Chicago on the plane, Tom and his mom had a long time – four hours- to talk about their visit in San Diego. He was glad he didn't have to fly that distance very often.

"So what do you think?" Tom asked. "Was it worth it?" He already knew the answer, though. His mom had been able to fulfill the dream of her own mother, which was finding her adopted daughter.

Emily laughed. "Silly question! Of course it was worth it. If only San Diego weren't so far away. Four hours on the plane and then another hour from Chicago to Springton."

"True," Tom said. "A long trip. So, were you surprised by anything as far as Angel is concerned?"

"Well, first of all our looks. I had never imagined we'd look so much alike. And then to find out she has a cousin in Springton. Hard to believe."

"Yeah, and it's good old Nate. Two very different people."

"And how was the golfing with Gary?" Emily asked.

"Very good, although the rental golf clubs left something to be desired.

I think I could have played better with my own clubs. But Gary is a nice guy. A real environmentalist."

Emily smiled. "Angel said he's trying to make big changes in their house. Like using fewer plastic bags and recycling whatever they can."

"I guess that fits," Tom said.

"I found out that Angel has been divorced for about five years. Another thing we have in common."

"Do you think you'll see her again?" Tom asked.

"I sure hope so. I invited her to Springton, and she said maybe later in the summer she could get some time off from her job."

"Good! And by then you'll be married to Franklin," Tom said. "Lots of good things in the future."

CHAPTER TWENTY THREE

KATIE

Consider it all joy, my brethren, when you encounter various trials, knowing that the testing of your faith produces endurance.
James 1:2-3

And we know that God causes all things to work together for good to those who love God, to those who are called according to His purpose. Romans 8:28

Spring had finally come to Michigan, Katie thought as she and Dan drove to church that third Sunday in April. The skies were blue, the temperatures were in the mid-seventies, the tulips were unfolding, and the car windows were down with fresh air gently floating in. Spring was a season of promise, she thought, looking over at Dan. For her it held the promise of their marriage, and starting over in a new city. It was everything good.

They turned into the parking lot and parked next to Tom, Franklin, and her mom, who were getting out of the car. Dan had suggested last night that it was his turn to be a visitor, and he wanted to visit her mom's church. Fine with her. She wouldn't have to worry about running into Angie. They all greeted one another and then walked quietly into the old red brick building with its tall white columns.

During the service, she wondered what Dan thought about this church. It was somewhat different from his. In his church the music, for example, seemed geared for a younger crowd. Here in her mom's church there was a choir, hymns, and an older crowd. She liked both, she decided, each in its own way. She could probably get used to either type of service. Another thing she and Dan could decide together in Mishawaka next fall.

The pastor had a good sermon. The theme of wondering about life's problems, and why we had them, was similar to this week's set of short stories in English class. She needed to re-read them this afternoon and be prepared for an essay tomorrow in class.

She listened more closely. People tended to say 'Why me?' when bad things happened to them, the pastor seemed to be saying. Why would a good and loving God allow really bad problems in our lives? Just like in the stories she was reading. The characters felt that since they were good people, why weren't they free of big problems?

It made sense to her until she heard the pastor this morning. Like if we never had problems, how would we know that God could solve them? If our lives were perfect, would we feel the need for God? And most importantly, the pastor said that God has a purpose for whatever happens in our lives.

At the end of the service, she, Dan, Tom, Franklin, and Mom followed everyone out to the sunny courtyard at the side of the church, where a group of high school kids were helping serve coffee, tea, and donuts.

"Excellent idea," said Dan as they all stood around enjoying the sweets. "Good move to have the young people be the servers. This is a great church," Dan said to her mom. "The pastor's sermon was very good. The subject is definitely on our minds sometimes."

"I suppose we've all wondered at times why God allows some things in our lives," her mom said. "But you, Dan, you've been so good for Katie. Thanks for being with us today."

"Hey, Tom," someone called. A young girl came up to their circle and smiled at Tom.

"Hi, Lori," Tom said. "Great to see you; I didn't know you went to church here."

"Actually I just started a couple of weeks ago," Lori said.

Then Tom introduced Lori to the group. Turns out she was a new nurse at the hospital. She didn't look that old, thought Katie. But she was very nice looking. And maybe just what Tom needs in his life? They all talked a few more minutes before Emily suggested they all go to a buffet restaurant not too far away. "And Lori, we'd love to have you join us if you're not busy," her mom said.

Lori glanced at Tom, who looked very welcoming, Katie thought. "Thanks; I'd love to."

Bingo, Katie said to herself. She hoped Lori would turn out to be good for Tom.

❋ ❋ ❋

The next day, in Katie's English class, the teacher divided the class into groups, telling them to talk about the themes in the three stories. Unfortunately the teacher used a different system to form the groups, so she found herself with people she didn't know at all. Except Luke. He was in the group. Great, she thought.

There were six of them. Luke seemed to stand out, at least in Katie's mind, because he seemed so different from the others. Was it all the tattoos? Was it the too-small sweatshirt with spots on it? Was it the hair that hadn't seen a barber's scissors in quite a while?

Maybe all of them, Katie thought. He was different, but he was there in the group, so she decided to not be so judgmental. Of course there was the fact that he had gotten drugs from Ralph; at least that was what she had deduced from his behavior at the book store, and from hearing him talk to his friends that one day outside of the classroom building. She remembered that Luke thought Ralph's prices were too high.

So the idea was to talk about similarities in themes among the three short stories. "Someone got in trouble in each story," one girl in a pink headband said.

"But they all seemed to be good people, basically," a guy in a red polo shirt said.

"So does that mean that people have problems even when they're good?" Katie wondered out loud.

"But what about the fighting in the one story?" another gum-chewing guy asked.

Then Luke spoke up, which surprised Katie. "Sometimes fights can happen when you least expect it," he said. "This character didn't go to that school room expecting a fight."

"Actually the fight didn't happen in a school in the story," Pink headband said. "Remember? It was at a bowling alley."

Katie glanced at Luke, who looked embarrassed. He was probably feeling sorry he had spoken up, Katie thought.

And sure enough, he didn't say anything more in the group. But she did overhear him talking to one of his friends on the way down the hallway after class. "I goofed up, said the fight was at school," he told his friend. "I guess I'm still thinking about Ralph. I really hit him hard."

"But that didn't kill him," the friend said. "In the newspaper it said he was killed with a knife in his neck."

The two turned down another hallway before Katie could hear any more. She shivered, which was odd on this nice spring day. Was that important information, she wondered? It sure sounded like it. She'd be talking to her mom that night, for sure.

CHAPTER TWENTY FOUR

FRANKLIN

Keeping away from strife is an honor for a man, but any fool will quarrel.
Proverbs 20:3

Do not say 'I will repay evil.' Wait for the Lord and He will save you.
Proverbs 20:22

Every man's way is right in his own eyes, but the Lord weighs the hearts.
Proverbs 21:2

Franklin drove into the school parking lot on Monday morning feeling a bit down. He didn't like feeling that way. He didn't want to feel that way. But there it was.

He turned off the motor and sat in the car. The day was sunny. Michigan clouds were gone for a while. He turned his head to the right and saw tulips lining the walkway into school. He was going to marry Emily in a couple of months. He got along well with her kids. They both agreed on important matters of God and church.

So why? Why feel down in the dumps? Maybe it was all because of Ralph, he decided. His death was hanging over his head like a cloud waiting to drench him with gallons of rain water. Someone had possibly used his very own knife to kill the man. No one knew for sure, but he wondered, since his knife was missing from the desk where he had always kept it. It wasn't as if he missed Ralph, who seemed to be cranky all the time. But Ralph was killed with a knife in his own classroom. How could he go on, look ahead, with that staring him in the face? This had to be resolved.

But that wasn't the only thing hanging over his head. He had always prided himself on his ability to get along with people. But now he wasn't getting along with Nate. Not good. What could he do? Ignoring it wasn't helping. Could he perhaps talk to Nate face to face? Apologize for not giving him the job of assistant golf coach? Tell him how much it made sense to have his assistant be in the same building with him, as he would be next year when he moved to the Freshman wing? Would any of that help at all? Maybe. Maybe they could at least be fellow teachers even if they couldn't be good friends.

❋ ❋ ❋

Franklin thought about his 'Nate' problem all day, or at least in-between classes. His history classes kept him busy discussing and listening to other ideas. Like Franklin Roosevelt getting elected four times as president. Was that good for the country someone wondered? He loved it when kids asked questions.

He mentioned to Pat and Emily at lunch that he might try to talk to Nate again. Pat wondered if Nate would even listen to anything. Emily encouraged him to try, saying if nothing else he would feel better. Which was true, he felt.

So as soon as the last student left after school, he locked up his room and walked over to the business hallway to Nate's room. He hoped to get there before Nate left for the day. He wasn't there, so he went to the business office. When he walked in, everyone was jabbering to each other. Franklin said 'hi' to several, and the room seemed to become quiet, he thought, as he went over to Nate's desk. Perhaps that was because Nate had been spreading untruthful rumors about him. Everyone in the room probably thought he was nuts even being there.

"Hi, Nate," Franklin said, trying to put on a cheerful face. He noticed that Nate was busy grading papers. "Sorry to interrupt, but would you have a couple minutes to talk?"

Nate looked up, surprise on his face. "Um, sure." He looked around, probably wondering if the small inner office was busy. "Let's go back to the little office."

As soon as they sat down, Franklin got right to the point. No exchanging little pleasantries about the weather, the hyper kids in the spring, or whatever. "Nate, I'm really sorry it didn't work out with the assistant coaching. It's mainly because Jeff works in the Freshman wing, where I'll be next year. It'll make the whole job so much easier."

"Well, thanks for coming to see me," Nate said, looking like he wanted to say something nasty. He paused. "I think you'll be sorry, though. I checked out Jeff's qualifications, and I know I'd do better."

Franklin didn't know what to say. He hadn't expected that. Luckily there was a knock at the door and Joanne from the Physical Education department came in.

"Hey, Nate, just wanted to see if we can have a conference about a student." She looked at Franklin quickly. "Sorry I interrupted. You know, it's uncanny how much you look like Ralph," she said, looking at Franklin.

Nate looked just as surprised as Franklin felt. "Are you kidding?" Nate asked. "Franklin here has a short neck compared to Ralph."

A short neck, Franklin thought. What an odd thing to say. "Uh, Nate, I'll leave you to your conference. Just wanted to smooth things over if I could."

Nate said nothing as Joanne just looked at him. So Franklin quickly fled the room. He walked down the hall to the main office to see if he had any mail. While there, Steve came in, also checking his mail box.

"Do you have a minute," Franklin asked Steve.

"Of course. Come on in to my office."

"So I've been feeling guilty about not choosing Nate," Franklin started. "I hated the idea of someone on the faculty having such animosity toward me. So I went to his office to apologize. I told him how much easier it would be to have my assistant be in the same building with me. And all he said was how much better he could do the job than Jeff could."

"That's no surprise to me," Steve laughed. "He tends to have a big ego. But it was big of you to at least try."

"Yeah, I guess. Not sure it did any good," Franklin said. "There is one odd thing. Joanne from Phys ed came in asking Nate a question, and then she looked at me and said I resembled Ralph. Weird. Nate just said that was crazy, that Ralph had a much bigger neck."

"Well first of all, I see absolutely no resemblance to Ralph," Steve said, chuckling. "But it is odd that he'd mention the neck."

"You know," Franklin said, "Nate mentioned the neck. Ralph was found with a knife wound in his neck."

"You're right."

Both of them were quiet.

"Someone who killed a man with a knife would know if that guy's neck was big," Franklin said.

Steve nodded. "For sure. I think, though, that I'll run all of this by Louie. Can't hurt."

"Okay, thanks for listening. I'll leave you to your work." Then Franklin left the office.

CHAPTER TWENTY FIVE

EMILY

Do not be wise in your own eyes; fear the Lord and turn away from evil. Proverbs 3:7

Do not fear, for I am with you; do not anxiously look about you for I am your God. I will strengthen you, surely I will help you, and surely I will uphold you with My righteous right hand. Isaiah 41:10

We still don't know about Ralph's murderer. I wish the police could go faster on the case. Who, I keep thinking, could have done this dreadful thing. I need to keep praying. Franklin and I have a definite wedding date – June 14. But we need to make some specific plans, soon. I don't want anything big. Just family and a few friends. It's exciting. My life is going to look so different soon.

It was a Tuesday in late April. Emily had just had an interesting discussion on To Kill a Mockingbird with her honors English 10 class. She had put the class into groups of four to discuss Miss Gates, a teacher in the book. Miss Gates was teaching about Hitler during WWII, and Miss Gates said this: "We American people don't believe in persecuting anyone." So the groups were to talk about the quote. Was it true that American people don't persecute anyone?

Emily was pleasantly surprised to see the kids in each group start talking and arguing right away. "Well, sure, today it's not like what the Germans did to the Jews back then," said one person. "But what about how some African Americans are treated today?" said another. "Yes," said still another. "There are more of them in our jails than any other group." A fourth person related a news story of a young black man who was jogging, and two white men shot him, claiming he was a burglar.

Once the class got back together, the main opinion seemed to be that some Americans did persecute others. One person pointed out, however, that not all were like that. What Emily liked to see was that everyone seemed to be engaged in thinking and interacting. After class Ellie, who had been negative about To Kill a Mockingbird earlier, said this on the way out: "I guess this book isn't so bad after all." Emily had just smiled, but inside she was dancing a jig.

❋ ❋ ❋

After school there was a staff meeting for all the teachers, in the music room. Emily got there a little early and happened to sit near Nate and another man from the business department.

"Sure hope this meeting is short," Nate said to those around him. "I've got lots to do."

"It's a busy time of year, for sure," Emily remarked. "Hey, Nate, I just met someone related to you last weekend."

"Really?" he questioned. "I don't have relatives in Springton."

"How about San Diego?" Emily asked. "Angel is the one I'm talking about."

"Oh, her," he said. "Yeah, kind of a cousin. She had a hard time getting through high school and just ended up as a hair stylist."

"Well, that's a good job," Emily said. "We certainly need people like that."

"I suppose. At least she was able to help me out recently, when I needed a little extra cash one week," Nate admitted.

Then he turned to his friend, obviously thinking that Angel wasn't worth talking about. His last comment made her wonder if that was why there was no money in the sophomore account. He was running short, perhaps. Maybe he had to pay Ralph too much money?

And he certainly didn't want to spend much time talking to her. He could have asked how she happened to meet Angel. After all, they were cousins. Maybe he actually felt a little guilty about the sophomore account.

⁂ ⁂ ⁂

That evening it was just her, Kate, and Tom for dinner, such as it was. She had decided on an old favorite – sloppy joes, plus a salad of course. They laughed and kidded each other as they put out place mats, plates, and silverware, and then sat down at the oak table in the kitchen.

"This is nice," Emily said. "Just the three of us. Starting in June Franklin will be here of course, and I'm glad about that. But still, this is nice right now. Things will soon be changing so quickly. Franklin here in June, and then Katie leaves in September for college with Dan. And what about you, Tom?" Holy cow, she thought to herself. What had she been thinking, or not thinking? She had been so wrapped up in other things that she had overlooked wondering exactly what Tom would be doing in the fall.

"Well, I've been pondering that," Tom said.

"Oh, Tom, I'm so sorry. I've been too wrapped up in other stuff," Emily said. "So what have you been thinking?"

"That's okay, Mom," Tom said. "As you said, a lot going on."

"So classes will be in Kalamazoo," Emily said. "You'll want to stay there, right?"

"Right. I haven't made any plans yet, but I need to get busy on that. I'll probably look on line first, and then go to Kalamazoo to check things out, see about a small apartment."

"Let me know if I can help, Tom," Emily said. "Like the furniture in your room here. Take what you want."

"Thanks, Mom. I may do that."

"And have you settled on exactly what classes you'll take next semester?"

"Yes, actually I have. I've got two history classes plus two more general ones on secondary education," Tom said. "I may be talking to Franklin more about history, since he's the expert."

Emily smiled. "He'll truly enjoy that, although I've never known him to say anything about being an expert."

Then Katie inserted herself. “Maybe I could take a couple of things also?” Katie asked.

“Of course. Whatever you need.”

Then Katie continued. “English class was interesting today.”

Emily’s ears perked up. She enjoyed hearing what other English teachers were doing.

“So we read three stories and in groups talked about themes,” Katie said. “Luke was in my group. He’s one of the guys who met Ralph in the book store one day. He’s the one who said his prices were high.”

“Oh, yes. I remember,” Emily said.

Katie went on. “Luke didn’t say too much. Until we talked about a story where there was a fight. He said that fights can happen when you least expect them. And then the biggie.”

Katie paused for effect. “He said the character didn’t go to that school room expecting a fight.” Katie stopped again. “But guess what? That story didn’t take place in a school; it was in a bowling alley.”

“Very interesting,” Emily said. “It makes me wonder.”

“Do you think Luke could be the one who hit Ralph?” Tom asked.

“Well, interesting,” said Katie. “I overheard him saying that he hit Ralph pretty hard.”

“And did he actually kill Ralph?” Tom wondered.

“All he said was that he hit Ralph. Somehow I don’t think he would have stabbed Ralph,” Katie said. “All he and his gang seemed to want was drugs.”

“But Ralph was stabbed,” Tom pointed out.

“What if there were two people actually involved?” Emily said. “Anything could have happened overnight.”

⁂ ⁂ ⁂

Emily couldn’t stop thinking about that conversation that evening. Even as she sat at the table reading essays, she would go back to their talk as she put a grade on each paper. She remembered Franklin talking about finding Ralph in the closet. The way he was sitting, apparently Franklin could only see a huge bump on Ralph’s forehead. It was only later, when the police came, that it was clear that Ralph had also been stabbed with a knife. What if Ralph was hit first and then left in the room. Then someone else came in the room later, found Ralph half conscious and decided it was a good time to just get rid of him.

She'd talk to Steve tomorrow she decided. See if he thought her idea was a little ridiculous.

❋ ❋ ❋

The next morning she ran into Franklin in the front office as they both picked up their mail.

"Hi, Franklin," she said, smiling at him. He looked nice in his khakis, blue shirt, and sports jacket. "You're looking like the next assistant principal of the Freshman wing!"

"I'll take that as a compliment," he said. "Want to grab a quick coffee with me?"

"Sure. And I've got a theory to run by you. I just asked Steve if I could talk to him for a few minutes after school." Emily paused. "Maybe you can tell me if it sounds logical."

They got their coffees plus Franklin's donut, and found a table in the faculty room. Then she told him about Katie's English class and what Luke said, along with her idea about the death involving two people.

"So does that sound idiotic?" Emily questioned.

"Not at all. I would imagine Steve and Louie would be interested in any ideas at this point. Also it goes with my conversation with Nate." Then he told her about apologizing to Nate and then Joanne coming in and saying he looked like Ralph."

"You know that's ridiculous," Emily said. "You don't resemble Ralph at all."

"Nate thought my neck was shorter than Ralph's."

"You're kidding. What an odd thing to say. And does that tell us anything?"

Franklin shrugged his shoulders, saying he had relayed that to Steve. "Hopefully the police are looking into it."

She also told him about her short conversation with Nate, about Angel. "He really isn't very friendly at all anymore," she concluded.

"You're right," Franklin said. "At least I won't see him very often once I start the new job."

"Franklin, I'm going to miss you so much," Emily said. "Of course I'm glad for you, but it won't be the same here. Like no breakfast or lunch with you."

He smiled and took her hand. "But we'll be together every night," he said. "And won't that be great!"

"You're right," Emily said. "Different, but better also."

CHAPTER TWENTY SIX

TOM

Trust in the Lord with all your heart, and do not lean on your own understanding. In all your ways acknowledge Him and He will make your paths straight. Proverbs 3:5-6

When Tom got into his car that April morning, the first thing he had to do was turn on the wipers to try to get all the snow off the windshield. No. Didn't work. He opened the back seat door to locate the scraper; it wasn't there. So he tried the trunk, and there it was, laughing at him. And you thought you wouldn't need me for a while, it seemed to say. Such fickle Michigan weather. The streets were fairly clear, though, he found as he drove to the hospital. At this time of year all the snow could disappear by noon.

By the time he parked, rode the elevator to the third floor, and walked to the nurses' station, Cheryl was there and waving him over.

"So glad to see you, Tom," Cheryl said. "We need some of your 'magic' on a patient."

"Bring it on," Tom said, smiling, and thinking how much he'd miss this place when he went to grad school at Western Michigan University in Kalamazoo in the fall.

"So the patient's name is Claire, in 314. Probably mid-50s. Liver Cancer. Early stages, but it doesn't look good." Cheryl stopped and looked at her notes. "She's halfway hysterical whenever the doctor comes in her room, asking if he really knows what he's doing. It's like she doesn't trust anybody."

"Odd," Tom said. "Has she said anything about past bad experiences with doctors?"

"Not really," Cheryl said. "To tell you the truth, I haven't been able to get her calmed down enough so she can even answer my questions."

Lori came up to the desk then. "So 'magic' man will do his thing?" she asked.

"I'm sure he will," Cheryl said. "He's really a miracle man."

"You know," Tom said as he started off. "I think I like 'miracle man' better than 'magic man.'"

They both gave him a thumbs-up.

"Whatever you say," Cheryl said with a smile.

Then Tom turned around. "I'm going to make a quick trip to the cafeteria. Be right back."

"Maybe this is the magical part," Cheryl said. "A cookie and Coke?"

Tom gave another thumbs-up.

As he walked to the cafeteria, he wondered if Claire would feel like eating anything. Well, he could always try. If nothing else, she would know that someone cared enough to think of her. And just in case, he asked for a plastic bag for the cookies. If she didn't want one now, maybe she would later.

When he got to Claire's room, she was watching Wheel of Fortune on TV.

"Hi Claire," he said. "I'm Tom, a nurse helper, just seeing how you're doing. And if you feel up to it, I've got cookies and Coke also."

She looked at him in a rather disinterested way and continued watching Wheel.

"So I see you're a Wheel fan. My Mom loves that show and sometimes I watch it with her."

Still no response. Well, he had time, he thought. So he pulled up a chair and started watching it also

"Oh, here comes the crossword puzzle," he said. "Those are fun. This one is moon_____. Hmm I wonder if one of the words could be 'light.' Think that would work?"

"Well, there is a place for a five letter word," she finally said.

Then a contestant guessed an 'L.'

"Yes, it's got to be 'light,'" she said, sounding a little more interested in talking.

After they watched a few more minutes, she reached for a cookie. "I guess I'll see if this will go down. And thanks for bringing them."

'You're welcome. I just like to help out where I can. And cookies always make me feel better," he said, chuckling.

By this time the show was over, so Tom decided to ask a question. "So how is everything going here? I see you've got a problem with the liver. That sounds tough."

"Yeah, it is tough. I feel so lousy most of the time, and the doctors here don't know what they're doing."

"Have you tried the Coke?" Tom asked. "That might be good with the cookie."

She took a sip and nodded.

"So what do you wish the doctors would do?" Tom asked.

"Get me out of here," she muttered.

"I would imagine they're hoping they'll be able to do that," Tom said.

"They don't act like it." She frowned. "It's just one test after another. And no one tells me anything."

"Have you got any family coming around," Tom asked.

"Not really. No parents, no husband. One son. But he's at WMU."

"At Western? No kidding. That's where I graduated, and I'm going back there to grad school in the fall."

She gave a slight nod, looking sleepy.

"I'll come back tomorrow, Claire. See how you're doing, ok?"

Another nod, and her eyes closed.

Tom went back to the nurses' station to report. "She mentioned lots of tests, and the doctors don't tell her anything, and she feels lousy. She did eat a cookie though."

"At least she talked to you," Cheryl said.

"True. And we watched Wheel for a while. Maybe you could check on what the doctors are telling her? I think she's depressed and lonely. She has a son at WMU, but he's in school now."

"Sure, I'll see what I can find out," Cheryl said.

"And I'll look in on her tomorrow," Tom said.

The rest of the day went by quickly. There were lots of patients who needed wheeling into surgery, or the x-ray room, or needed help to walk for a few minutes. At one point he had time to take a short break in the cafeteria. He got in line for a ham sandwich, paid for it, and looked around for a vacant table. Then he spotted Lori.

"Mind of I join you," he asked, coming up to her table.

"Of course. It's always good to see 'miracle man,'" she said, smiling.

"So how is the hospital treating you?" he asked. "Is this your first job since school?"

"So far it's great, and yes, first job."

"It was good to see you at church," Tom said. "Everyone enjoyed meeting you and talking over lunch."

He paused, taking a bite of his sandwich.

Then she started talking about church. "I've really liked the pastor's sermons. I've noticed how he'll talk about a passage I've read before, many times, but he brings something new to it. Something I had never thought of before."

"Same here. I've had the same experience," Tom said. "And he really seems passionate about whatever his topic is." Tom took a sip of Coke and went on. "I was going to say I'd be missing him when I go to grad school, but I'm thinking I'll be coming home on many weekends. He's that good."

"Grad school? What will you be pursuing?"

So he told her about changing his goals from being a family doctor to getting a secondary teaching degree with a major in history. "It may take me a couple of years to get all that done, but I feel sure it'll be worth it." Then he looked at his watch.

"I guess I'd better get back before Cheryl thinks I abandoned her," he said, getting up.

"Me too." And she stood up.

They walked back together, and Tom made a decision before they reached the nurses' station. Would she be up for a dinner this weekend? She grinned; she would. He smiled too. He liked the thought of getting to know her better.

❋ ❋ ❋

That night after work he went home ready to change clothes and relax before meeting his dad for dinner. Apparently his dad had met a client near Springton, so he had time to meet Tom before heading back to Chicago. Tom was glad for the chance to talk. Jack had left in a huff the last time he saw him, after accusing his mom of not doing anything for their kids. Which was ridiculous of course. His mom? Are you kidding? She did everything she could do for her kids. But it was an awkward moment. He and Katie had talked about it later and both wondered if their parents would ever get along. Sometimes he just couldn't understand his dad.

Dinner that night with Dad was pleasant. They talked mostly about sports. Once in a while in the past Tom had brought up a patient, and how he handled a situation. But honestly his dad never seemed very engrossed in those conversations.

Near the end of dinner, as they were finishing up their steaks, his dad mentioned his grandpa's house. "So it actually sold last week. We'll be closing soon."

"That's good news, right?" Tom asked.

"Absolutely. But I just wanted to check with you," Jack said, sitting back in his chair.

"You're really okay with me giving it all to Katie? Not that she doesn't deserve it. I just wanted to make sure."

"Dad, I would really love for Katie to have it. My patient last year gave me a lot of money. I'll be able to pay all my school bills, and that's what I want for Katie." Tom was sure he had shared the patient gift before, but again, sometimes he felt his dad wasn't listening to him.

"Okay," Jack said. "It's good to know you two won't have lots of money problems."

"And thank you, Dad," Tom said. You've been very generous." It was true, Tom thought. He was being a good father.

"Dad, there is one thing that would make Katie and me even more happy."

"Oh? And that is?"

"If you and Mom could get along. I couldn't ask for nicer parents. But sometimes we feel bad when we see conflict."

His dad was quiet. The waitress came up and asked about dessert. They both shook their heads no. His dad paid the bill, and they left the restaurant to walk to their cars. Tom wondered if his dad would just ignore the request, maybe even pretend he hadn't heard it. Were his parents that far apart? Sure, they were divorced. But if they could see that ongoing conflicts hurt the kids, wouldn't they consider doing something differently?

Tom reached his car and turned around, ready to thank his dad for dinner. Instead, Jack put his arms around Tom.

"Sometimes you give very good advice for a young whippersnapper," he said.

Tom laughed as his dad went to his car, waved, and drove away. You just never know, he thought, if you're saying the right thing. And he silently thanked God as he drove home.

⁂ ⁂ ⁂

When he opened the garage door and went into the house, he found his mom and Franklin in front of the fireplace talking. He could hear the word Nate as he walked in.

"Hi Mom, Franklin," he said, sitting down in a side chair. "Any news about Ralph's murder?"

"Not really," Emily said. "I did talk to Steve about my theory. That maybe two people had been involved in the killing. He felt it was worthwhile talking to Louie about it."

"Good," Tom said, all of a sudden feeling tired. Lots had happened that day; it was time to unwind. "I hope it's solved soon, as you do too of course. I suppose everyone at school is talking about it."

"And how," Franklin said. "We keep finding out how many people disliked him or held a grudge against him."

"Interesting. Well, see you later," Tom said, standing up. "Another busy day tomorrow."

"Night, Tom," his mom said.

⁂ ⁂ ⁂

He woke up the next morning thinking of Claire. He wondered how she was feeling, and if she had been able to eat anything.

At the hospital, he asked Cheryl about her.

"I did get a chance to talk to the doctor about Claire," she said. "He said he'd definitely talk to her in detail about her situation, right after he runs more tests this morning."

"Thanks, Cheryl," he said. "I guess I'll wait until later to see her; I'll try to time it for after her doctor talks to her."

"Good plan," she said.

There was no problem keeping busy the rest of the morning. And then he and Lori timed their lunch break so they could eat together. Which made Tom happy.

"So I happened to go into Claire's room this morning," Lori said.

"Oh good. How was she?"

"She had two visitors. One seemed to be a pastor, I thought. They were telling her something that I had never heard before."

"Really? What was that?" Tom asked. He had the impression that Lori had gone to church since she was a little kid, so he wondered what this pastor could have said that would sound so different to her.

"He told her that she must not have enough faith; otherwise she'd be cured by now."

Tom looked at her in disbelief. "Not enough faith? As if God answers all of our prayers the way we want? As if God takes orders from us?"

"I know. I can't believe it, either. And I wonder how she'll feel after the doctor talks to her today," Lori said, "because Tom, I think she's getting worse, fast."

Tom's heart sank. If she was depressed and lonely before, what must she feel like now? Curious about Lori's thoughts, he asked what she thought about that pastor.

"I don't know what church he represents," Lori said. "But it's nothing like what I've been taught. We pray, of course, but we ask for God's will in the answer. Sometimes His plans are different from ours."

"Exactly,' said Tom. "That's what I've heard also." He was glad that they were on the same page with that essential belief.

When they returned from lunch, Tom asked Cheryl to let him know when the doctor talked to Claire. "I have a feeling it might be important to see her after the doctor tells her about the test results."

Cheryl nodded in understanding. "In that case, you could go to her room now. The doctor has been there for a while. Maybe he's gone by now."

"I'd like to do that," Tom said, "unless you need me here."

"No. Go ahead. She may need you the most."

So Tom went to Claire's room, opened the door quietly, and saw that she was alone. The doctor obviously had left. He walked in and found her looking out the window.

"Afternoon, Claire. Am I interrupting anything?"

"No, no. Come on in. Especially if you have a cookie." She smiled, although Tom could see tears in her eyes.

"Hang on," he said. "I'll come right back."

It only took him a few minutes to race to the cafeteria for cookies and Coke. In a way he was surprised that she wanted them.

He went in her room with the tray of treats. This time she was sitting up in bed, but hooked up to oxygen.

"So how are you doing?" Tom asked as he moved the tray near her so she could grab a cookie by herself.

"Well, I don't know," she said. She ate a bite and was quiet.

Tom sat down, wondering if she'd want to talk, and hoping his presence wouldn't bother her.

"I'm going to leave here," she finally said, in a whisper. "To hospice. I'm not getting better. I guess my pastor was right. I don't have enough faith."

Tom moved his chair closer and took her hand. "Claire, do you believe in Jesus, that he died on the cross for you, that he wants to help you in all of this?"

She nodded.

"Then you do have enough faith. No matter what, God will never leave you. God has a plan for you. He's watching over you, and He wants to comfort you through this." Tom took out a small notebook from the pocket of his jacket and turned to one of the verses that had always helped him. "Do not fear, for I am with you; do not anxiously look about you, for I am your God. I will strengthen you, surely I will help you, surely I will hold you with My righteous right hand." (Isaiah 41:10) "By the way, Claire, you know God is going to heal you, don't you?"

"He is?"

"When you get to Heaven, you'll be all perfectly healed. It'll be wonderful."

She gave him a small smile. "Thank you, Tom. You've been such a comfort to me."

"Is anyone calling your son? Or could I help with that?" Tom asked.

"Oh, would you? I know I need to talk to him, but I don't know if I can right now."

"I'll be happy to. Does the nurse or doctor have his number?"

She nodded and closed her eyes. Tom patted her hand and left the room. He'd make the call, for sure, but he hoped he had been able to give her some comfort. She must feel so alone.

CHAPTER TWENTY SEVEN

KATIE

Never pay back evil for evil to anyone. Respect what is right in the sight of all men. If possible, so far as it depends on you, be at peace with all men. Romans 12:17 – 18

It was May 1, a day that should have been sunny, bright, and in the 70s. It wasn't. Cold, rainy, and in the 50s. It was to be expected in Michigan, which was known for having fickle weather. Katie knew all this, but still she sighed as she turned up the thermostat to get warmth into the car. She had to hurry; she didn't want to be late for English class.

Her mother had talked to her last night as she was reading the three-story assignment. Again, they were to look for common themes. She thought she had a handle on it: life wasn't fair; people change. She could see either one as being important here.

"Katie?" Emily knocked gently on her door. "Could I bother you for a minute?"

"Sure, Mom. Come on in," Katie called. "I'm just reading my stories for tomorrow."

"Anything good?" Emily asked.

"All of them. This teacher really has such an interesting class."

Emily looked at the story titles and nodded her head. "I recognize these. It's good to hear that her class is a good one. But I have something else on my mind. Luke."

"Luke?" Katie asked, wondering if this had something to do with Ralph.

"Right. I told Steve what you related to me, about him maybe having a fight in a school room." Emily paused. "I'm not sure, of course, but the police may have talked to Luke."

"Ah," Katie said. "Makes sense. So you want me to be careful."

"You've read my mind. I'm probably being silly, or over-protective. A mother never stops worrying, you know." Emily laughed. Then she went on. "The thing is, Louie found Luke's name and phone number on Ralph's phone. It looked like a list of people who owed Ralph. So the police would likely have talked to Luke even if you hadn't heard anything suspicious in class. I thought it important that you know that."

Katie stood up from her desk and hugged her mom. "Thanks, Mom. I'll watch out."

Her mom left with a wave as Katie sat down and finished reading.

⁂ ⁂ ⁂

So now she was driving to class in the rain, wondering if Luke would be in her group again. She parked at school, got out her flowered umbrella (a present from Mom) and walked to class. She put her dripping umbrella on the floor beside her desk and looked around. No Luke. Yet. She chatted with the girl next to her about the stories and then saw Luke slink in just as the teacher started talking. His ratty sweatshirt was all wet and he looked like he could use a razor.

The teacher asked them to group up with the same students as last time. Some groaned, and the teacher said they'd form different groups next time. Katie wanted to vote for that idea.

The girl in a headband, blue this time, spoke first. "It seems to me that one idea is that life isn't fair. The boy in the drug store was accused of stealing, and he hadn't. In fact, he saw someone else leaving the store without paying."

"It's never fair to be accused of doing something you didn't do," Luke said.

The group was quiet for a moment, thinking it over. Katie thought his comment was interesting. What could he have been accused of?

"That's a theme, true," said the guy in a polo shirt, green this time. "But I also saw changes in characters."

"What do you mean?" gum chewer asked.

"Well, in one story, the girl didn't understand what being poor was all about until her dad was laid off from the car factory."

"Good point," Katie offered. "She didn't seem to look down on the poor like she had before. She used to assume that being poor was all that person's fault."

"And what about the story where the guy tried to cheat playing golf in a high school golf tournament," Luke said.

Katie looked at him, surprised. Two comments in one class so far!

"Oh yeah," blue headband sad. "He did change after that. When he didn't win, the coach talked to him privately and told him he'd never win by cheating. So he stopped."

"At least when no one was looking," gum chewer sad.

"I thought he really did change," Luke said. "It's possible you know."

Katie noticed Luke glancing her way as he spoke. Did he want her to know something?

They talked more and then the teacher had them write a short essay about a theme in the stories.

After class she was walking down the hall to the exit when Luke came up beside her.

"You saw me in the bookstore with Ralph," Luke said in an accusing tone.

Katie could feel her heart skip a beat. She glanced around. They were all alone for the moment.

"Did you tell the police about that day?" Luke asked.

They were at the exit now. She reached out to push the door open, but Luke pulled the handle toward them.

"Luke, I never talked to the police," she said, which was true. She had talked to her mom, but not the police. "Why would I?"

"Ralph was dealing in drugs," Luke said. "But you probably guessed that."

Katie was quiet, wondering how she could get around him. What did Luke want? What did he expect her to say? "Uh, Luke, I need to get home."

She could hear a quiver in her voice.

"Just a minute. Hear me out."

She looked at him. Why? Why did he wat to talk to her?

"I bet you think I killed Ralph."

She looked at him in horror. Why wasn't anyone coming down the hallway?

"I didn't," Luke went on. "I did go to the classroom to find him. I shoved him when he called me a lying druggie, after I told him I'd have the money soon. He fell into the bookcase, hit his forehead pretty hard. But I didn't kill him. Please. You've got to believe me."

"Okay," she finally whispered.

"The police may talk to you. But I've learned a lesson. I've changed. I've learned what drugs can do, not just to the body, but to the mind also. Like the people in those stories. I wish you'd tell them that."

She nodded her head. He pushed the door open for her just as a group of students came near. She walked quickly to the car, got in, and locked the door. She was shaking. She thought back over the scene at the door. It was so unbelievable. Why did he care what she thought? And would the police care what she thought? She guessed he wanted her to tell the police that he had changed. But how did she really know that? It seemed ludicrous.

After class Katie drove to the bookstore. She was scheduled to work for four hours that afternoon, although she didn't really feel like it. What she wished she could do was go home, hide under the covers on her bed, take a long nap, and forget about Luke. He had scared her so much. But he said a couple of times 'I've changed.' Had he? Or was he just saying that so she'd give a favorable report to the police, that is if they even contacted her. The truth. She hoped he was telling the truth. How could she know?

She had hoped she could talk to Dan about all of that, but he was busy all afternoon and she didn't want to bother him. In the middle of her shift a policeman came into the bookstore. She was alone at the cash register; Buddy was in the back taking a break.

"Katie Sanderson?" the policeman asked.

She nodded. Here it comes, she thought. He's going to ask her about Luke.

"I'm Louie; I've talked to your mom and Steve at the high school about the circumstances around Ralph's death."

Suddenly Buddy was there. "Katie, I'd be glad to work here so you can talk somewhere private," he said.

She gave him a grateful smile, and she and Louie went to the reading corner, which was empty. Actually the whole store was quiet, probably because it was near the end of the semester.

Louie then asked her about her recollections of seeing Luke with Ralph in the bookstore, and then about what she overheard after class recently.

"So, I'm just following up," Louie said. "We're not accusing Luke of anything; I'm just collecting all the facts I can."

Louie seemed very kind. Here she was talking to a policeman. That had never happened to her before, ever. She should have been scared to death. But he had a way of just calmly trying to get information.

"There is something more," she said hesitantly. Then she told him about the class, how they read stories and talked about themes. "One story was about people changing," she said. "And Luke told the group that it was true; people really could change."

She paused. Should she tell him more? Tell him about Luke talking to her after class? Yes, she should, she decided. Louie waited patiently as she thought it through.

"So after class, Luke followed me to the exit. He asked me to believe him, that he didn't kill Ralph, and that he had changed."

"Okay," Louie said. "Anything more?"

"Yes." She thought back to that scene. What else did he say? "He said he had gone to see Ralph at school because he needed more time to get the rest of the money he owed Ralph. But Ralph called him a lying druggie. That's when Luke pushed him and he fell against a bookcase."

"That's consistent with what we've got so far," Louie said.

Katie went on. "But Luke said he didn't kill him. I don't know how he knew for sure. Maybe he felt his pulse? I'm not sure. Anyway, the last thing he said to me this morning was this: I've changed, please believe me. I know now how bad drugs are."

"Thanks, Katie; you've been a big help," Louie said as he left.

She was left wondering. Had she done the right thing? Could she believe Luke? And did people really change?

That evening was pizza night. Her mom had invited Franklin and

Dan, also, which was great, Katie thought. It made her feel so good that Dan seemed to like everyone and fit in so well.

While Tom and Dan went to the Pizza Shack, Katie helped her mom put out paper plates, knives and forks, napkins, and Cokes on the kitchen table.

"Guess who visited me today while I was working," Katie said. "Well, I guess visit isn't exactly right. He asked questions."

"Must have been Louie," Emily said. "Did everything go okay?"

"It did. I was nervous," Katie admitted. "No experience with the police, you know."

"Which is a good thing." Emily chuckled.

"He's a nice guy. He was patient and put me at ease."

Emily smiled. "Glad to hear it. I've been impressed with the way he handles students, also."

The door slammed and the guys came in with three boxes of pizza.

"Wow," Katie said. "We can really chow down."

Franklin came in from the living room where he had been watching the news; he said a prayer, and then they all dug in.

It was quiet while everyone ate and enjoyed the meal. Then Katie decided to ask the question she'd been thinking about all day.

"So, gang, I have a question for you."

Everyone lifted their heads and looked at her, so she went on. "Can people change; I mean really change from doing questionable things to doing things right?"

"Of course," Emily said.

Franklin, beside her, was nodding his head also. "With God, anything is possible."

"Well," Katie said after a pause. "I'm not sure God played a part in this, at least from what I can see."

"But don't we, as Christians, need to give someone the benefit of the doubt?" Tom questioned. "God can help us, who are Christians, change, but a non-Christian can change, too. Things can happen in our lives that make us see that we're doing something wrong."

Katie nodded thoughtfully.

"And another thing," Dan interjected. "We need to be forgiving like Jesus forgave us." Dan stopped and walked over to the coat rack. "I've got something that might help. Just read it this morning." He took a small Bible out of his coat pocket and brought it to the table.

"You can tell Dan's going into the ministry," Franklin said. "He comes prepared with a Bible."

Dan smiled. "You just never know when it'll come in handy." He flipped through a few pages. "Okay, this is from Colossians 3:12-13: 'So, as those who have been chosen of God, holy and beloved, put on a heart of compassion, kindness, humility, gentleness and patience; bearing with one another, and forgiving each other, whoever has a complaint against someone; just as the Lord forgave you, so also should you.'"

"This must have something to do with Luke, in your class. Right?" Emily asked. "I don't blame you for questioning, but like Tom said, and Colossians, we need to give people the benefit of the doubt, and forgive."

Katie looked around the table with gratitude. She loved her family so much. She reached for Dan's hand and gave it a squeeze. God was so good to her. And she'd pray for Luke, that his change would be permanent.

⁂ ⁂ ⁂

The next day was filled with both studying and working at the bookstore.

Buddy kidded her about the policeman. "I was hoping I'd see you again, that you hadn't been arrested."

They both laughed. "The police are still working on that school custodian case," she explained. "One of the people possibly involved is in my English class. But I'm pretty positive he's not the murderer. Oh, by the way, thanks for taking over so I could talk to him. I was pretty nervous, so that helped.

"No problem," he said.

⁂ ⁂ ⁂

Once she got home there was another surprise. This one was in the mail: a check from her dad. At first she just stood there, stunned. It was for more than she had imagined: two hundred thousand dollars. Holy cow, she thought. This was from her grandpa's house. She had had no idea it would be this much.

Tom came home from the hospital as she was sitting at the kitchen table looking at the check in amazement. He smiled when he saw it. "This will be so good for you, Katie. Now you can finish school without big money worries."

"I'm really grateful," Katie said. "To Dad and to you. You gave me your half, which was so incredibly generous of you."

Tom gave her a hug. "Now study hard, little sister." He smiled and wandered off to change his clothes before dinner.

After dinner Dan came over, and they went out to get ice cream at the local dairy bar. She told him about the check, and was surprised at how quiet he became.

"Katie," he said. It looked like he was trying to find the right words. "I had it all planned out; we don't have to use this money. Maybe you'd like to save it?"

She looked at him, puzzled. "I thought you'd be happy. Now I have money for tuition."

He was quiet a moment. "Of course I'm happy. But shouldn't we get jobs too?"

"Oh, yes. I agree. We can still do something part time. But this money will help take some of the worry away. Don't you think so?"

Dan took a bite of ice cream, apparently thinking. "Everything will be just fine," he said.

And they went on to talk of other things.

❋ ❋ ❋

That night, after she got ready for bed, she put on her robe and trotted down the hall to her mother's room.

"Hey, Mom, got a minute?"

"Of course. Take as many as you want," Emily said with a smile. She finished washing her face, sat on the edge of the bed, and indicated that Katie should sit also.

"So what's going on?"

"I told Dan about Dad's check," Katie said. "He didn't react like I thought he would."

"So what did you expect?"

"I guess I thought he'd be happy."

Her mom sat quietly, thinking. "He probably had things all worked out in his mind? I mean about how to pay for everything?"

Katie nodded. "True."

"I think maybe you need to be patient here," her mom finally said. "Have your money ready to be used, but let Dan kind of be in charge of when it's needed."

"Really?" Katie asked. "Like does he feel he's less of a man somehow?"

Emily smiled. "Well, I don't know as I'd go that far. Just be careful. He wants to feel like he can be the provider for you. He'll realize in time what a help that money is. Just go slowly."

"Like don't 'lord' it over him that I've got all we'll need, or that I'm better than he is?"

"Something like that," Emily agreed. "We'll pray about it. Let God lead the way."

Katie left her room feeling better, and relieved. Things would be okay with her and Dan. But she needed to start praying about problems like this. Why hadn't she thought of that herself?

CHAPTER TWENTY EIGHT

FRANKLIN

> I will lift up my eyes to the mountains; from where shall my help come? My help comes from the Lord, who made heaven and earth.
> Psalm 121: 1-2

Franklin was standing outside his room beside the open door, watching students in the hallway come and go, put notebooks and backpacks in and out of lockers, and generally call out to all their friends. Steve encouraged the teachers to do that, in-between classes, as a way of calming students down and perhaps even stopping an argument or two. Franklin did it whenever possible, just because he enjoyed talking to the kids and bantering back and forth. Sometimes a student would open up to him outside the classroom, where he would never talk otherwise.

It was happening today. Rich was in his history class this hour, and he stopped to bend Franklin's ear about an assignment.

"So you asked us to write our end-of-the-year essay on something different if we could," Rich said as he stood next to Franklin.

"That's right; I did," Franklin said. "Have you thought of something?" He had wondered if the assignment might be greeted with dismissive groans or even flat-out no's. Granted, it was rather vague. But that seemed to appeal to some students. Many still needed help with topic ideas, and that was okay too. But it was fun to see if anything different would come up.

"I did think of something," Rich said. "You talk about golf a lot, and I wondered about looking into all the presidents who have golfed."

Franklin's eyes lit up. "Really? Great! Sounds very promising. I guess I don't even know who the first president on the golf course was."

"I checked it out on Google last night. It looked like it was Howard Taft in 1897."

"Hm… Interesting. Suggestion. Once you've done some research find a theme among the presidents. Like some common element in golfing style or how they used presidential time to do it. Or something like that."

Rich looked interested. "I'll give it a try," he said.

"Come back if you have some questions," Franklin said.

By then it was time for class to start. Franklin went into the room smiling, and not just because he liked golf. It was fun to see kids think of different ideas. Yes, he'd miss this teaching next year in the assistant principal's office.

❋ ❋ ❋

At lunch that day Franklin enjoyed a hamburger as he talked with Pat and Emily. He told them about a possible paper on presidents playing golf.

"Sounds interesting," Emily said. "Was that your idea, since you love golf so much?"

"No, not really. Rich in second hour seemed to think I had talked about golf a few times, though. Hard to imagine. Anyway, that's where his idea came from."

The two women laughed.

"So he talked to me today. Said since I do mention golf occasionally, he wondered about researching presidents who play golf."

"It might be fun to read," Pat commented. "It seems like most of our presidents have played golf, haven't they? And speaking of golf, weren't you teaching Jose's son how to golf?"

"I am. He's coming along. Not the greatest, but he's learning," Franklin said. He finished his hamburger and took his napkin to wipe his fingers and mouth.

"Will he be on the golf team?" Emily asked.

"That's what I'm debating. He's not a great player, as I said, but I do need a couple more on the team for back-up."

Emily thought a minute as she ate her salad. "Could you work with him some more this summer? I bet he'd improve by fall."

Franklin nodded. "Could be. And I feel like I need to give him an extra chance. He's had a lot going on with his mom and her citizenship, or lack thereof, and his grandma dying in Mexico."

"I'm sure that would mean a lot to Jose," Emily said. Then she cleared the table of trash and walked it over to the barrel.

"But Marco did try to steal your computer," Pat said.

"True. But he apologized and wrote a paper for Emily." Franklin looked at Emily and smiled. "I honestly feel I can trust him."

Franklin checked his watch. "Time to go back." He turned to Emily. "Are we still on for dinner tonight? I'll cook."

Pat's eyebrow went up and Emily laughed. "Which means we'll go out somewhere. And that's fine. See you later."

❋ ❋ ❋

After his last class, Franklin closed the door and looked at all the quizzes he had collected that day. He had time, so he decided to tackle them now. Maybe he wouldn't have to take anything home.

He was making great progress when he heard a quiet knock on the door.

"Come in," he called.

Jose came in quickly, looking as white as a newly bleached sheet. He walked in, closed the door, went over to Franklin's desk, took something out of his pocket, and placed a knife on the desk.

Franklin's eyes opened wide. "What's going on? Oh, is this mine? Where did you find it?" Franklin looked it over. Yes, it was the very one he had always kept at the back of his desk drawer.

"It was in Nate's room. I know Ralph was killed with a knife; I heard you were missing yours. Anyway, I decided to come to you."

"Okay. Good. But Nate's room? You're kidding. Where was it?"

Jose was quiet a moment, as if trying to calm down. "Well, he told me he needed help getting books out of the closet. So I brought a ladder and started hauling them off the shelves. Then he had to go to a meeting, so I kept working. After I had all the books off the shelves, I reached back to see if I had gotten all of them. I felt something on the empty shelf, but not a book. It was a knife."

"Holy cow." Franklin sat down and told Jose to sit also.

"I didn't know what to do," Jose continued. "So I came here."

"Okay. Let's think here. I guess we should get right down to Steve's office," Franklin said, thinking some more. "I'll wrap up the knife and fill up my briefcase with these papers, and put the knife at the bottom. Then I'll follow you to the office."

Jose nodded, got up, and left the room, closing the door behind him.

Franklin found some paper towels in his closet and wrapped the knife, although it might not matter. There'd be so many finger prints on it by now. Then he stuffed it and the papers in the briefcase. He stopped to think a minute. Anything else? No. So he opened the door, turned around to lock it, and saw Jose. On the floor, face up, with blood coming out of his forehead.

This can't be happening, he thought. Not someone else. Was he dead? Please, God, don't let him be dead. He knelt and felt a pulse. He took out his cell phone. Called Steve.

"Steve, Jose has been hurt, badly. He's on the floor outside my room, bleeding from his head."

"I'll call 911 now and be right down."

Franklin sat down on the floor and put his head in his hands. And prayed. Prayed that the paramedics could get here fast.

"Franklin?"

He looked up to see Emily walking down the hall.

"I was going to ask you what time . . ." Then she saw Jose.

"Franklin, what happened?"

Franklin shook his head. "This is what I just saw when I came out of my room. I called Steve; he's calling 911."

Steve came running up next. He stopped, looking horrified at the scene. "So the ambulance is coming to the exit at the end of the hallway. Hopefully soon."

"Any idea what happened, Franklin?" Steve asked.

Then Franklin told both of them about Jose's visit just minutes before. And about the found knife.

"Oh, my gosh," Emily said. "I don't know if this means anything."

"What? What is it?"

"I was walking to your room. When I turned the corner I saw Nate walking very fast the other way. He had something long in his hand. Then he went into the library."

By this time the ambulance had come up to the side door. Two paramedics quickly walked in with a stretcher and put Jose on it. "We'll take him to St. Joseph ER," one said to them. "Does he have a wife, and can you call her?"

Steve nodded. "I'm Steve, the assistant principal. Thanks for your help, and we'll take care of the call."

They left and Steve motioned them to follow. "Let's go to the office. I'll call Jose's wife. Louie too. And we'll talk about all of this."

It didn't take Louie long to arrive. Franklin gave him the knife and explained that Jose had found it. Then they each told him what had just happened after school. Louie had to answer his phone so he left the office to talk.

"That was a nurse from ER," Louie said, coming back into the room. "He's going to be okay."

They all sighed with relief.

"Did he need stitches?" Emily asked.

"Yes. Quite a few, actually. He was hit with something small and very hard."

Franklin and Emily looked at each other. They had wondered what Emily saw Nate carrying down the hallway. Could it have been a golf club? Could the end of the club make an injury like that?

Louie went on. "So I asked the nurse if the doctor could tell what kind of object had hit Jose. She called the doctor over and talked to him."

Louie looked at everyone quietly. "I asked him if there was any way he'd be able to tell if it were a golf club hit. And he said that he had been thinking that very thing, oddly enough. By the way, Franklin, I've heard you're a big golfer. When I go to look at Nate's golf clubs, is there one in particular I should concentrate on?"

Franklin thought a moment. "Interesting question. I think I'd inspect the 9-iron first."

"Okay," Louie said. "And Emily, you said you saw Nate carrying something long. Can you think of anything else?"

Emily frowned and tried to concentrate. "No, I'm afraid not. It all happened so fast."

"I'm calling for some back-up here," Louie said. "We'll look at Nate's room, and talk to him also. It could take a while, so you're free to go now."

After Louie left, the three of them tried to put together a scene of what could have happened that afternoon. Franklin looked at his watch. Close to 5:30. "Should we go get a bite somewhere and talk this over some more?"

Steve and Emily both nodded their agreement. Franklin suggested the River Café, thinking it might be quiet and wasn't too far away. They each took their own cars. On the way over Franklin was feeling good that they liked his suggestion. There was no way he could go home and do anything normal after all this excitement. Talking it over seemed like the thing to do.

Once they ordered and the waitress brought their drinks, Franklin started it out. "First of all, if Nate actually did all this, why would he hide the knife behind some books?"

"I was wondering the same thing," Steve said. "You'd think he'd go to some big dumpster and throw it away. Or maybe go bury it in the woods outside town."

"I suppose he could have thrown it there, thinking he'd get it later. Do you suppose he just got to the end of his rope with paying Ralph the hush money?" Emily asked. "Maybe Ralph had even raised his rates."

"Makes sense," Steve said. "So he looked for a quiet time, after all the teachers and students had left the building, to go confront Ralph."

The waitress came up then with a tray full of food. She passed it all around and they started eating.

Then Franklin added to the scenario. "So he found Ralph in my room, thinking he'd just confront him with the unfair money arrangement."

"But Ralph was already knocked out," Emily said. "Maybe he thought this was a good time to get rid of him permanently."

"But how would he do it?" Steve asked. "No gun, I'm sure. So he must have looked in Franklin's desk."

"And he found my knife. The police said the wound wasn't large. It would fit my knife, I'm afraid," Franklin said.

Then Steve went on. "So he stabs Ralph and sits him in the closet."

"And lucky me. I find him the next day, although I don't see the knife wound because he's facing the closet door."

"So now he has to figure out what to do with the knife," Emily said. "I suppose he could have put it in his pocket and gone to his room looking for a place."

"It still doesn't make sense to put it in his book cupboard," Franklin said. "Why didn't he take it home and get rid of it?"

"What if someone starts to come into his room as he's deciding all of this?" Steve asks. "He could have just thrown it in the closet and opened the door for this person."

"Makes sense," Emily said. "And then temporarily forgot it was there?"

"He must have," Franklin said. "Because he asks Jose to bring a ladder and help him get all the books out. And Jose said he left for a meeting, so Jose was alone when he finished the job and found the knife."

Steve took over with the possible scene. "So while Nate is in the meeting, he remembers where he had thrown the knife and he runs back to his room. Jose is gone. The knife is gone also. Now he really has a problem."

"Interesting that he came to my room to look for Jose," Franklin said. "I guess it was no secret that we were friends, especially with me teaching Jose's son Marco how to golf. So maybe that was just a lucky guess for him."

"He must have heard Jose talking to you, so he waited outside your room," Steve said.

"And then hit Jose with the golf club when he came out," Emily said. "He must have been feeling quite desperate about that time."

At that point all three of them decided it was time to finish their sandwiches, so it was quiet for a few minutes.

"I wonder if Louie found Nate while we've been talking," Franklin said. "It's hard to know if he'd find that club, or anything else suspicious in his room."

"Well, I'm sure he'll get back to me tomorrow," Steve said. "I guess I'd better be getting home. See you two tomorrow."

After he left, Emily and Franklin ordered some pie and ice cream to share. Neither one felt like rushing home.

"So what do you think?" Emily asked. "Have we solved the crime?"

"You know, I really think so. But we have to wait and see if Louie agrees."

"Well," Emily said. "We did our best. "I'm just sorry there had to be something like this happen in our school. Whoever would have thought there'd be a killing, and in your classroom. It's just very sad."

Franklin nodded. Yes, it was sad. No matter what anyone thought of Ralph, it was hard to believe that anyone wanted him dead. Unfortunately, it looked like Nate did.

CHAPTER TWENTY NINE

EMILY

Sing praise to the Lord, you His godly ones, and give thanks to His holy name. For His anger is but for a moment, His favor for a lifetime; weeping may last for the night, but a shout of joy comes in the morning. Psalm 30: 4-5

As the Bible verse says, joy comes in the morning, and I'm starting to see it. We're working on helping Jose's wife get her citizenship; Jose himself is healing after his attack, and their son Marco is finding joy in golf. Two weddings are coming this summer, which gives me much joy. Tom is finding the path for his career. And we're close to finding out who finally had enough of Ralph and got rid of him. All around, there is much for which to be thankful.

Emily was in the office Friday morning getting her mail, which turned out to be just the usual daily announcements and excused absences list. Nothing earth-shaking. She checked her watch to see if there was time to go to the cafeteria for an iced tea. She was early, so tea it was.

Suddenly she heard Nate's name being mentioned. She turned to see Lois, who was a regular substitute teacher in the high school. Lois was asking the secretary for a key to Nate's room. Interesting, Emily thought. Nate was absent today. What did that mean? Flu? Or maybe Louie talked to him yesterday and discovered something?

"And I think I'll be here at least a week," Lois was saying. "Should I just keep the key until the last day?"

"Sounds fine with me," the secretary said. "After all, you're such a regular here. Just see me if you need anything else."

Curious, Emily thought. She left for the cafeteria, got her tea, and went to the faculty lounge.

"Oh good," she said as she saw both Franklin and Pat at a table with their coffee. She sat down and whispered. "Guess who I just saw: Lois. Here subbing for Nate for at least a week."

"No kidding," Franklin said after he swallowed a bite of his chocolate donut. "That really is news. Also that explains Steve's text to me this morning. He asked if the two of us could meet him in his office after school."

"So I take it that there's progress on Ralph?" Pat asked.

Franklin nodded. "Yep. And I'm assuming progress about Jose as well." Then he told Pat about Jose getting hit and being taken to the hospital.

"Good heavens," Pat said. "This school is fast becoming a scary place to work. No wonder you're eating another donut."

Emily laughed. "Right. Any excuse at all will do."

Franklin finished his donut. "But it works, you see. I'm feeling much better now. Totally equipped to handle all those kids."

"And speaking of kids," Emily said. "We'd better scoot."

⁂ ⁂ ⁂

The rest of Emily's day went smoothly. When she unlocked the door to her room, everything was just as she had left it the night before. She opened her closet, and it was filled with a sweater and books. No dead body. Good start. And considering it was a Friday, the students were mostly on-task and cooperative that day. Couldn't ask for anything more.

Well, okay, there was one problem. She caught one of the girls in her English 10 Regular class cheating on a To Kill a Mockingbird quiz. She usually walked around class during a quiz, so it wasn't hard to see Annie coughing several times and reaching inside her pocket for a Kleenex, and then looking at the Kleenex quite carefully. So after class she asked Annie to stop at her desk before she left the room.

"I'd like to see the Kleenex in your pocket," Emily said, trying to stay calm and cool.

"Why? There's nothing wrong," Annie said. A tell-tale flush was coloring her face as she spoke.

Emily just stood there quietly looking at her, not arguing. Annie seemed to be getting more and more nervous.

"I have to go to my next class," Annie finally said.

"Sure, as soon as you give me the Kleenex."

Emily then moved to the side, shutting the door so students from next hour wouldn't come in yet.

"Well?" Emily said. "Shall we talk about this? Or should we go to the office?"

"Oh, gosh," Annie said, slamming the Kleenex on the desk. "It's just a stupid quiz, and I forgot to read last night."

Emily picked up the Kleenex with several words written on it. "Did you know that I don't give the same quiz to my classes? So these answers didn't help."

Annie looked at her, clearly embarrassed. "Can I go now?" she said rudely.

"This situation won't go any further if you do something for Monday. Read the chapter and write a summary. And apologize also."

Annie looked shocked.

"Please don't let that happen again. Cheating is not the way to get ahead in life." Then Emily opened the door and many students burst in the room, and Annie ran out in-between them.

Emily sighed as she put the quizzes in her briefcase and straightened her desk. She wondered if Annie had learned anything. She made herself a note to follow-up on the situation Monday and make sure Annie did what she was asked.

The last hour of the day was good from beginning to end. No cheaters. That was nice. First they had a discussion on mockingbirds. She had asked them to find out what kind of bird it was and even bring in pictures if they could. After that the students paired up and wrote a paragraph on how Tom Robinson was like a mockingbird. This was an honors class, so she was confident they would think beyond looks and contemplate the situation Tom was in, his personality, and how he was treated. Several read their paragraphs, and they were good. One student – Jeremy – seemed to sum it up well. "Mockingbirds sing and don't do anything wrong; they're not pests, and they aren't game birds to stalk and kill. People lied about Tom just because he was black. He wasn't treated right. Also I think Miss Gates in the book wouldn't have liked Atticus defending him."

❋ ❋ ❋

Franklin showed up after the students trailed out the door. "You're smiling," he pointed out.

"I am. Some good discussions on To Kill a Mockingbird. And how was your day?"

"Also fine. I'm anxious to hear what Steve has to say."

"Me, too," Emily said. She picked up her purse, locked the door, and they walked to the office.

❋ ❋ ❋

Steve was waiting for them in his office. "What a day," he said sighing. Some good and some bad."

"So let's hear the good first," Emily suggested.

"Jose's wife is getting a chance to get her citizenship, and it looks good for her. As reported by Louie," Steve added.

"Awesome," Franklin said. "Such good news for Jose."

"And the bad news?"

"Looks like Nate won't be back to school," Steve said.

Emily and Franklin looked at each other. Louie definitely had made progress yesterday.

"So what happened exactly?" Emily asked.

"First Louie checked his room. Found no golf clubs. He did find a list in Nate's desk drawer. A list of payments to Ralph. The blackmail had been going on for quite a while, and the amount of money kept increasing."

"We wondered if maybe Nate finally got fed up with Ralph's greed," Franklin said.

"Looks like it," Steve said. "So then Louie got a search warrant and went to Nate's house. Fortunately Nate was there. They found the golf clubs, finally. Nate had them in the trunk of his car."

"Nate must have been furious by then," Emily said.

"And how," Steve said. "Nate had quite a few nasty things to say to Louie."

"So did the golf clubs have anything on them?" Franklin wondered.

"Yes. Louie and the policeman with him went over them very thoroughly," Steve said. "It was the 9-iron, just as the Franklin suggested, that finally showed just a little blood, even though it was obvious that the clubs had been cleaned."

"And were they able to match it with Jose's?" Emily asked.

Steve nodded. "Yep. So Nate was arrested this afternoon on assault charges."

"But what about Ralph?" Franklin asked.

"They'll be very intensely questioning him about that. I feel confident that they'll be able to get Nate on murder, also. After all, thanks to Jose, they have the knife now, which was found in Nate's classroom."

"So the end of the mystery," Emily said. "Or is it totally? They still have to prove that the knife is the same as the one that killed Ralph."

"True," Steve said. "But I'm confident that will be done. Leave it to Louie."

"I sure hope so," Emily said.

"At some point there will be a trial of course. Some of us may be called to testify. I guess it's sort of over, but not quite," Steve said.

"It's just too bad," Emily said.

Both of the men looked at her, questioningly.

"I mean Nate had it made. A good job, for example. But he let anger get to him. How did he think he'd solve his problems this way?"

"I have no answers, I guess," Steve said.

They all rose from their chairs, and Steve thanked them for coming in.

"Oh, there is one other thing. I'll be talking to the superintendent about how to handle this with the staff. So in the meantime, let's not say too much."

Emily and Franklin nodded and then left.

❋ ❋ ❋

On the way out of the building, Emily asked Franklin to come over for dinner. "I'll see who'll be at home for eating; maybe this would be a good night to run down to the Sandwich Palace."

"Sounds good to me," Franklin said.

"Oh, one more thing," Emily said. "I've been thinking about Angel, my sister in San Diego, and cousin to Nate." Emily stopped, not sure what she was actually thinking. "I guess I'm wondering if I should call her about what's going on."

"You know, that might be better than learning about it in the papers," Franklin said. "I'm sure it won't be an easy thing to talk about, but I think she would appreciate it in the long run."

"Thanks, Franklin. I think I'll call her tonight or tomorrow."

They each went to their classrooms to pick up briefcases; then they left.

Tom's car was in front of the house when Emily got home and pulled into the garage. She walked in the door and found him and Lori sitting at the kitchen table drinking Cokes and talking. It was a nice scene, she thought. It seemed so natural, as if they had been doing this for a long time.

"Hi Lori and Tom," she said as she set her briefcase in the hall and then sat down. "And how was your day?"

"Great," said Tom. "One of my patients, Claire, had her son come to town from Kalamazoo, and he was with her as she got settled in a hospice location. She seemed so much better, and at peace." He stopped a moment. "That's why I love the job. It's great to talk to people and help them calm down, or even just listen to them. And I think I was able to help Claire with her questions about faith; that's really important to me."

Then Lori spoke up. "I can see how Tom got the reputation of 'miracle man,' just from the short time I've been there."

Emily smiled; the mother in her loved hearing how much her son mattered in the hospital. "Thanks, Lori. I agree. By the way, Franklin is coming soon. We're thinking of ordering take-out, maybe sandwiches. You two are welcome to join us."

"Thanks, Mom," Tom said. "But we're planning on going out." Both he and Lori stood up. "But thanks for the invitation. And by the way, I'm going to check on an apartment in Kalamazoo tomorrow. Lori is going with me to give her approval."

"Good news, Tom. And good to have someone along to help inspect."

Emily waved at them as they went out the door. It was nice to see her son going out with someone as pleasant as Lori seemed to be.

Katie and Dan were the next to come in.

"You're just in time," Emily said, "that is if you want to eat a sandwich with us."

Katie and Dan looked at each other. Which told Emily all she needed to know.

"Mom, I think we'll pass this time. We're going out for a major talk," Katie said.

"Major?" Emily smiled. "How interesting."

"It is. Definitely. First, though, we have to ask you if this date works: September 2.

"Perfect," Emily said. "I'm assuming we're talking about wedding plans?"

Katie laughed. "You're so smart."

"You know," Emily said thoughtfully. "That was my parents' anniversary date. Looks like that would be the perfect date for you two. So now go have your major talk, with my blessings!"

Katie hugged her mom. "Okay, Mom. See you later."

Franklin came to the door as they left. "Hi Emily, do any of the kids want to eat with us?"

"Not really. Each of them seems to have other plans tonight."

"Then it appears to be just you and me," Franklin said. "And that's not all bad."

"A sign of the times. The kids are grown up and leaving the nest."

"That seems to be God's plan," Franklin said.

Emily smiled, feeling very contented. She had found someone special, and her kids appeared to be headed that way too. It was everything good.